OUT OF COURT

OUT OF COURT

CHARLES BUTLER

BOXTREE

Dedication:
For Josephine

First published in the UK 1992
by BOXTREE LIMITED, 36 Tavistock Street,
London WC2E 7PB

1 3 5 7 9 10 8 6 4 2

ISBN: 1 85283 697 0

Typeset by DP Photosetting
Aylesbury, Bucks

Printed and bound in Great Britain by
Cox & Wyman, Reading, Berkshire

A catalogue record for this book is available from the
British Library

Chapter One

Tribeca's Restaurant was crowded and humming, full of L.A.'s Best and Most Beautiful. The decor was hi-tech baroque with a chromium stairway that ended in a jungle of exotic plants. At a table in an alcove, below a fat golden cherub who was fighting to escape from a mass of purple drapes, Ann Kelsey and Stuart Markowitz were preparing to leave.

'Thank you, Stuart – that was wonderful!' she gushed, taking his arm. Behind them the chubby *maître d'*, with a two-inch satin stripe down his trousers and a stack of gold-embossed menus under his arm, bowed unctuously.

'The best part,' Markowitz said, ignoring the man, 'is that we get to go home together!'

'You're right about that,' said his wife, turning to smile briefly at the *maître d'*; but as she did so, the smile froze on her lips. 'Oh my God!' she gasped, looking beyond the *maître d'*'s shoulder.

'What?' Stuart said, starting to turn and follow her stare.

Ann said quickly, lowering her voice, 'Don't make it obvious. Just nice and slow – to your immediate left.'

'Is that nice and slow enough?' he asked, trying to walk

1

straight and twist his head round at the same time. He managed it, just long enough to get a glimpse of Leland McKenzie, Senior Partner of McKenzie Brackman and Partners, who was sitting at a nearby table, in another draped alcove. he was dining *à deux* with none other than the notorious Rosalind Shays – the high-powered attorney who had recently sued the Partnership for wrongful dismissal, and won a quarter of a million dollars . . .

'What the hell are they doing?' Markowitz cried, his eyes bright with the thrill of gossip.

'What does it look like they're doing? – they're having dinner,' his wife snapped, hurrying him towards the door. She didn't think Leland and Shays had spotted them – yet.

As Stuart skuttled along behind her, he kept straining to get a further look behind him. 'Social? It couldn't be social . . .?' he said excitedly. 'You think it's social?'

'They're sitting in a booth, stupid! Why would they choose a booth unless . . .?'

As they reached the doors of the restaurant, Stuart took a last look back. He was in time to see Leland lean forward across the table, take Rosalind's hand and give it a little kiss.

*

Douglas Brackman opened the Morning Conference with his first smile of the day – he allowed himself four.

'First up – a very happy birthday to Arnold Becker!'

Becker looked distinctly uncomfortable, even angry. 'My birthday isn't till Thursday, Douglas.'

'Agreed. But since you seem to be particularly anxious about it, I thought I'd make it a point to remind you every day this week.'

'This the big four-oh?' said Jonathan Rollins mischievously.

'Thirty-nine,' Becker said grimly. 'Can we move on, please.'

Brackman consulted the list in front of him. 'Now here *is* some good news. I am sure we'll all be happy to congratulate Leland here on landing Velnick Industries – a major manufacturing company of household fixtures, and a client which could guarantee us billables upwards of a quarter of a million dollars, annually.'

'Fantastic!' Becker cried. Ann Kelsey shot her husband a sly glance, knowing that this plum prize in the Partnership's lap was more due to the Rosalind Shays connection than anything that old Leland McKenzie could have drummed up on his own.

Leland, meanwhile, acknowledged the congratulations of his colleagues with deadpan modesty, his eyes cast downward behind his bifocals. And again Ann Kelsey wondered if she oughtn't to broach the matter with McKenzie. After all, it was a matter of *trust*.

'And *more* good fortune,' Brackman boomed on, unusually upbeat for him, as he looked now at Becker. 'I see, Arnold, that you have a meeting with Christina Sheppard, regarding her divorce from Leonard Bey, the Chief Exec. of Kenmore Consolidates.' Douglas Brackman managed to invest the subject of divorce with all the glutinous glamour of a prime suckling pig at Christmas time.

Becker took his cue. 'Yeah – this could be major. Mr Bey is worth fifty to a hundred million. Hopefully I'll reel Ms Sheppard in this morning.' He made her sound like a prize King Salmon.

3

'Let's hope so,' said Brackman sharply. 'It's been a while since you've brought in a big one.'

Becker bristled. 'What are *you* bringing in, Doug?'

'It was just an observation,' Brackman said stiffly. 'Don't be so sensitive – during your birthday week, too!'

McKenzie gave him a short, reproving glance. 'Douglas!'

'Sorry,' said Brackman. 'We're adjourned.'

*

Christina Sheppard was one of those young, naturally beautiful Californian women who graduate from the casting-couch and pornographer's lens, through to a series of husbands with sturdy bank accounts and weak hearts; and, if all else fails, resorts to the bare-knuckled cunning of the best divorce lawyer in town.

Christina entered Becker's office just ahead of him, trailing a discreet aroma of the best scent on the market. She did a graceful half-turn in the middle of the floor and sat down in the client's chair, crossing a pair of legs that would make an archdeacon do cartwheels down Sunset Boulevard.

She smiled, as Arnie settled himself carefully behind his desk; then said, in a gentle, matter-of-fact voice, 'I'm not going to lie to you, Mr Becker – even though I happen to be quite good at it. You're the ninth lawyer I've gone to. The other eight all said the prenuptial agreement can't be broken – which is terrible because it limits me to half a million.'

'And you want more?' Becker gulped, trying not to look at her legs.

'Much more. Leonard's worth about seventy million

4

dollars. So five hundred thousand seems rather modest – even trivial.' Her smile was soft, dazzling.

'Maybe,' Becker said cautiously. 'On the other hand, you've only been married to him for seven months.'

'Quality time. Look, I made a mistake – a mistake I'd like *him* to pay for – and I hear you're very creative.'

Becker swallowed hard. 'Let me look over this agreement and see what I can come up with. Four hundred dollars an hour,' he added drily, 'applied against a non-refundable retainer of thirty thousand.'

Her smile chilled a little. 'That seems high – compared to the others.'

He grinned like a wolf. 'I don't compare to the others, Ms Sheppard.'

'Is that right?' she said, in a deep husky voice that made his spine tingle.

'I'm going to assign three lawyers to comb through this little contract of yours, Ms Sheppard. And you're going to tell me everything you know about your husband. *Everything*, whether you think it matters or not. Then I'll get to work – making you a very large amount of money. How does that sound?'

She gave him a smile that said it sounded fine. Just fine! And said a lot more, too. Becker thought he might start sweating any moment, if he were the sweating type, which he wasn't. Instead, he smiled back – the true Becker smile. Christina Sheppard and he were gonna get on just fine, he was thinking.

*

Becker's next appointment with her was for noon the

following day. Although he wouldn't admit it, even to himself, he'd spent just a little longer than usual that morning preparing himself: he'd shaved with especial care, making sure he didn't leave any tiny nicks or abrasions and applying a double spurt of New West aftershave, and had chosen a pale blue shirt with dark blue polka-dotted silk tie that showed up his blue eyes to their best advantage, topping it off with a matching silk handkerchief sprouting nonchalently from his breast-pocket. Every inch the whizz-kid L.A. divorce lawyer. Arnold Becker was serious; he was in charge, and he meant to keep it that way.

He had been in his office most of the morning, boning up on what line he was going to take with the gorgeous Christina Sheppard; and had just gone out into the open-plan complex to get a drink from the water-cooler – smoothing down the quiff of blond hair to cover his very slightly receding brow – when he saw his wife, Corrinne, approaching Roxanne's desk. He stopped, just in time – before either of them saw him . . .

Corrinne was looking very pretty, in a tight skirt that showed up her neat little behind. 'Hi, Rox!' she called. 'How we doing?'

'*We're* doing fine,' Roxanne said, looking mildly irritated. Corrinne was spending too much time hanging round the office these days; she never wasted an opportunity to pop in, on some flimsy excuse, to see if Arnie was all right. Make sure he was taking lunch – bringing him sandwiches, a little smoked salmon, perhaps, even a thermos of her own fresh-brewed coffee. Roxanne knew she should feel a little sorry for the woman, but these persistent visits still annoyed her. She had a law office to run, for Chrissake. 'Arnie's sulking in his office – he's really freaked,' Roxanne went on, just out of his earshot.

'That's why a surprise party is just what he needs,' Corrinne said brightly. Still neither of them had noticed him by the water-cooler. 'He's working too hard,' she added. 'I'm worried about him . . .'

Becker heard this and came forward. 'Worried, honey?'

Corrinne covered her surprise with a smile. 'Hi sweetie! I just dropped by to say hello –'

'Uh-huh?' – he sounded suspicious – 'You two cooking up something? Because in case you're planning any kind of surprise party, you can forget it. I'm not celebrating this birthday.'

'We'll got out to dinner!' Corrinne beamed. 'Just you and me.'

'No,' he scowled, 'I have to work late Thursday night.' He looked at his watch: 11.55. Five minutes to blast-off. Only, with a woman like Christina Sheppard, she'd almost certainly be late. 'Have to run . . . Sorry.'

He turned awkwardly, avoiding both women's eyes, knowing he was being ungracious but not being able to help himself. Just then Jonathan Rollins appeared. 'Ah, Arnie. Been looking for you.' He held a stiff official-looking document out to Becker. 'This pre-nup agreement for the Sheppard lady – sorry, Arnie, the thing's air-tight.'

'Don't tell me that. I've been through it twice myself – and anyway, they haven't invented an air-tight pre-nup.'

'They have now,' said Rollins. 'This thing is crafted.'

'You're telling me this five minutes before the meeting?' Becker said, frowning angrily.

'I've been telling you since last night, Arnie – but you keep sending me back to –'

7

'Forget it, Jonathan. Just forget it!' Becker hesitated, glancing nervously at his wife and Roxanne, who'd both been listening to this. 'I gotta go to the bathroom,' he blurted suddenly; then turned to them both at the door. '*No parties*. Okay?'

Rollins watched him disappear; then shrugged and walked away. Corrinne looked anxiously at Roxanne, 'He's not himself, Rox.'

'Oh he's himself all right,' Roxanne said, 'it's just the new case in his life. The Sheppard woman, she's got to him.'

Corrinne still looked worried. 'What'll we do about the party? I already called the caterer.'

'Relax, honey. We'll just do it here.'

'Here?'

'If we can't get him to the party,' said Roxanne, 'we'll bring the party to him.'

Mrs Arnold Becker smiled uneasily. 'That's pretty dirty, isn't it?'

Roxanne grinned back, 'Like you said, Corrinne – Arnie needs this.'

Chapter Two

Leland McKenzie and Ann Kelsey entered McKenzie's office together. The Senior Partner was looking preoccupied, and perhaps a little anxious.

'What can I do for you, Ann?'

'I thought, initially' – she was choosing her words carefully – 'I wouldn't say anything. Only the more I think about it . . .' She straightened up, facing him across his desk where he'd already sat down, 'Stuart and I had dinner at Tribeca's the night before last, Leland. As we were leaving, we saw you kiss Rosalind Shays.'

He stared at her blankly for a moment, over his bifocals. 'Uh-huh,' he said slowly.

'That's it?' she said, 'Just "uh-huh"?'

'I didn't know my social life was any of your business, Ann.'

'It is if it affects the firm,' she said defiantly.

'It doesn't affect . . .' he began; but she cut in, beginning to sound heated:

'Leland, you had us represent her in that Tannenburg Trust suit because of your involvement with her. And that, in my book, Leland, amounts to deception – if not an outright lie.'

McKenzie's face had grown taut, pinched round the mouth. 'We represented her to save ourselves three hundred thousand dollars. It had nothing to do with . . .'

'Aw, come on!' she cried, 'Then why didn't you just say you were seeing her, Leland?'

For a moment a flush crossed McKenzie's drawn features. 'Ann, if *you* were having an affair with Rosalind Shays, would *you* tell anybody?'

'So you *are* sleeping with her?'

'Please leave, Ann,' – his voice was quiet and tight with fury – 'now.'

She took a deep breath. 'I don't trust that woman. I didn't trust her motives when she was here. And I certainly don't trust them with you now. What's more . . .'

'I said leave.'

It was her turn to flush. She clasped her hands in front of her, gave him a last determined stare, then swung on her heel and marched out. *Now I've done it*, she thought – accused the Senior Partner to his face of deception, even lying, all on account of a woman she'd never been able to stomach. Of course Leland would say it was personal. And who was to say he wasn't right? Supposing it *wasn't* any of her business after all? She was beginning to wish she'd held off a little longer. Yet for the good of the firm . . .

Ann Kelsey returned despondently to her room. She thought of calling on her husband and talking it over with him. But Stuart was always the same. He'd prevaricate, try to see both sides, and finally side with Leland because, deep down, he was scared of Leland – scared of all authority –

and he'd take the soft option of saying Leland's private life was his own business, and no-one else's.

Damn Leland. *Damn them all!*

.

*

There were four of them in Arnie Becker's room. Christina Sheppard sat poised like the Queen of Sheba, in a plain dove-grey linen suit that fitted her flawless body like a glove and left nothing to the imagination; to Becker's practised eye, across the desk, she might just as well have been naked.

At the end of the desk was Christina Sheppard's husband, Leonard Bey: a compact well-built man, heavily tanned, who looked as though he worked out in the Athletic Club. There wasn't an inch of flab on him, and his clothes had that solid, unobtrusive quality that spoke of real money; on his tanned wrist, half-concealed by a silk cuff, was a flat square watch of pure platinum. He wore lightly shaded sunglasses with steel rims. He was happy now to leave the talking to his lawyer, Mark Cleland.

Cleland was one of those tough, baby-faced Californian lawyers with a beach-shirt open several buttons to reveal a chest of wiry grey hair that matched exactly the hair on his head, and a lot of gold chains and bracelets that clinked when he moved, like a Roman centurion. He wore flared white trousers, little shiny black loafers with a gold chain across the the tongue, and dark glasses. He looked as though he might start calling everyone 'baby', if the mood was right. It wasn't. The jaw in the baby-face stuck out pugnaciously and his voice was like granite pebbles being rubbed slowly together.

He was saying, 'Quit stalling on us, Mr Becker. There is

11

nothing, absolutely nothing, that can shake this agreement, and you know it.'

'Bullshit,' Becker said calmly. 'It's so fundamentally unfair, it has virtually no chance of . . .'

'Five hundred grand for seven months!' Cleland snapped. 'I think she gets off pretty good!'

'Given your client's net worth, Mr Cleland, this contract is unconscionable,' Becker retorted grandly.

'She was represented by Counsel – this thing is binding –'

'But ambiguity is construed against the drafter,' said Becker.

'Very true. But there's nothing ambiguous about it.'

There was a faint, dry sizzle as Christina Sheppard languorously crossed one long leg over the other. Becker pretended not to notice. He went on, 'There's enough to get it into Court – where things can get very ugly, and that's something . . .'

'Is that a threat, Mr Becker?' It was Leonard Bey who spoke now, in a low pleasant tone that didn't need to get tough.

Becker hesitated. 'I'm not sure. The line between "threat" and "promise" is so easily blurred.'

'Go ahead – sue,' Bey said. 'I'll cross-claim her for being a gold-digging malicious slut.'

Not a line, not a muscle on Christina Sheppard's face had changed; she might have been sitting in church listening to a Monteverdi requiem for all the emotion she showed.

Cleland said, 'All right.' Becker just nodded. He said, 'We'll add for slander,' keeping the big handsome man in his sights.

Leonard Bey glanced at her and shrugged. 'I'm surprised at you, Christina. This is all you can come up with?' – and gestured across the desk at Becker, as though he were a garbage-bag.

Cleland came in smoothly, like a dangerous cat, 'All right. Let me tell you what I'm gonna do. In exchange for you recommending to your client that she walk away with the five hundred grand *and not a penny more*, I'll recommend to *my* client that he not haul you up on sanctions for abuse of process, frivolous prosecution . . .'

'And who the hell do you think you're talking to?' Becker yelled, in genuine fury.

'A lawyer who has no case, that's who,' Cleland said, with a tight little smirk.

'Do some research, Mr Cleland. You're dealing with Arnold Becker here.'

'Oh-oh?' said Leonard Bey, feigning terror.

'You're right,' his lawyer came in. 'Instead of the five hundred, we'll give you four.' And he and Bey laughed together, like a double-act.

Too quick, thought Becker. *They're beginning to crack already. All mouth – all wind and water.* 'Fine,' he said, 'we'll see you in Court.'

Cleland was smiling now. 'Hey, you know she's hired every lawyer in town to crack this. Doesn't that tell you something about the validity of this prenuptial? As for you, Becker, you're her ninth choice. That says something, too.' With a jangle of gold, he turned to Leonard Bey, 'C'mon, Lenny. We're dealing with Arnold Becker!'

Again they laughed together, and stood up. Leonard Bey squared his shoulders and looked down contemptuously at Becker, behind the desk. 'You didn't do your research,' he said; and they both walked out.

Becker hadn't moved. Nor had his client, Christina

Sheppard. After a moment she moved a slender, perfectly manicured hand and smoothed it slowly along the line of her thigh down to her bare knee. It's rare for a woman to have a beautiful knee, thought Becker; but this woman did.

'Look,' she said at last. 'Why don't you just bill me for the time spent, and we'll leave it at that?'

'It's not over yet,' Becker growled; he was still angry.

'For us, I think it is. It was nice to meet you – you're a very nice man.' She paused, hesitating, 'But I think I need –'

He looked at her coldly. She hadn't struck him as being a quitter. Far too cool and composed for that, surely? He met her eyes and said, 'I haven't finished with him yet, Christina. And you're not *firing* me. Give me another day. I can beat these bastards.' He gave her a hard, thin smile, 'And I'm *not* a nice man – I promise you!'

She sat looking at him for a long, slow moment; then she smiled. It was a lovely smile. It was a smile that made his legs melt under the desk.

*

They met again two days later. Becker was ready this time – trim and determined. He wasn't worried about shaving cuts or whether his quiff was in the right place. He meant business. And Christina Sheppard was late.

He met her outside the open-plan complex where he'd been waiting for the last ten minutes; he wasn't going to sit around alone with those two *schmucks*, cooling his heels for her in the conference room, where this second meeting was taking place. *Yessir* – today he was ready, fully briefed, prepared for a fight.

'You're late,' he told her. 'Where the hell were you?' –

and as he took her arm, he caught the faint scent of sandalwood.

'This better be good, Arnie!' she said, smiling. Today she was wearing pure white, under a little polka-dotted white jacket.

'Just play along, Christina. Don't *crumble*,' he said, leading her briskly into the conference room.

Leonard Bey and Cleland were already there, seated at the top of the big polished table. Neither of them moved as Becker and his client came in. Becker's jaw was set as he led Christina to the other end of the table, sitting down beside her. 'Gentlemen,' he said, with a short nod.

Cleland's baby-face was set like a lump of well-scrubbed stone. 'I gotta tell you, Becker – this time I *will* move for sanctions if . . .'

'This is *my* meeting,' Becker interrupted, 'and I'd appreciate it if . . .'

'Yeah, well just be glad we turned up,' Cleland said jauntily. 'Now let's just settle this right here and now. And I don't want to hear any more garbage about breaking the deal.'

Too fast, thought Becker again; *he's rushing his fences.* 'Oh, I don't care about the pre-nup, Mr Cleland,' he said airily. 'We're gonna be seeking an annulment to the entire marriage.'

Cleland gaped at him, while Leonard Bey's jaw dropped open half an inch. 'An annulment?' Bey said, in his low voice which was no longer pleasant.

'You gotta be kidding,' Cleland said, when he'd managed to collect his wits.

'No, I'm not kidding,' Becker said smoothly. 'Your client induced this woman into wedlock through fraud.'

15

Christina Sheppard gave him a quick glance, 'Arnie, I –' she began, and he silenced her with a ferocious glare.

Bey's jaws had snapped shut. 'What are you talking about?' he said, his quiet voice tense with anger.

'I'm talking about your inability to consummate this marriage naturally, sir. I'm talking about your penile implant.'

'His *what*!' cried Cleland.

Christina Sheppard's head had dropped. 'Oh, God,' she murmured.

Becker went on, 'I have to state now that my client had no knowledge that a material part of your anatomy was inflatable, Mr Bey.'

'She knew it!' Bey said, his voice rising for the first time.

'*It inflates?*' Cleland broke in, with a small disbelieving gasp.

'*After* you were married,' Becker said to Bey, 'and she never would have known, had one of your cylinders not ruptured.'

'Oh, for God's sake!' Bey yelled, his face turning white under the deep tan.

'What is this crap?' Cleland screamed, now thoroughly thrown.

'This crap, Mr Cleland,' said Becker, 'concerns an integral mechanical device designed to give your client an artificial erection.'

'Wait just a second?' Cleland cried, his voice both hoarse and shrill at the same time. He turned to Leonard Bey, 'You're not impotent, Lenny!'

'Absolutely not!' Bey said defiantly, 'I function, and I'm . . .'

16

'With the help of technology – yes,' Becker said icily, 'but . . .'

'All right! All right!' Cleland cried desperately; and beside him, Leonard Bey growled menacingly, 'You son of a bitch!'

Becker gave him a brief nod. 'Thank you. This goes directly to the issue of conjugal relations and is, therefore, grounds for annulment.'

'Is he kidding?' Bey said, turning to his lawyer.

'Quiet!' Cleland snapped. He was thinking hard, now that the full implications of Becker's discovery were sinking into his agile mind. 'Okay,' he said at last, looking at Becker levelly down the length of the table. 'You want an annulment – you got it. But that means they were never married – which in turn means that instead of five hundred grand, she's entitled to absolutely *nothing*!'

'Excellent point,' Becker said, stretching himself in his chair; he didn't look once at Christina Sheppard. 'Only thing is, for the annulment I'll have to file the grounds with the Court – and that, gentlemen, will make it a matter of public record that the Chief Executive of Kenmore Consolidates has this built-in body pump that shoots liquid into his . . .'

'That's blackmail!' shrieked Cleland.

Becker looked darkly at Leonard Bey. 'Two million dollars, Mr Bey – or the whole world finds out you're a self-made man' – and for a moment he thought he heard Christina Sheppard give a little titter beside him.

'You can't get away with this!' Bey roared.

'Oh yes I can,' Becker said, and he began miming a grotesque pumping action with his hand, pursing his lips and giving short sucking sounds.

'You can't do this!' Bey cried, his anger dissipating into pure horror.

'I will do it,' Becker said. 'Two million dollars by the end of business tomorrow!'

Leonard Bey suddenly jumped to his feet and, without looking to right or left, stormed out of the conference room. Cleland, left behind, sat staring at his adversary, his tanned face looking grey. 'Who the hell do you think you are?' he said, in a voice as friendly as a snake's hiss.

'Her ninth choice,' said Becker; and he sat back, basking in the rapturous gaze of Christina Sheppard.

Chapter Three

Conference began next morning five minutes early. The whole firm was there, with the marked exception of Leland McKenzie. They were all in their places when he entered. The atmosphere was charged, as though with electricity; the silence complete. He could sniff the lynching posse the moment he came in.

'What is this?' He stopped abruptly at the door. 'What's going on?' he demanded.

Douglas Brackman was staring down at the table. 'I have nothing to do with this,' he said, without looking up. 'I only just found out.'

Beside him, Stuart Markowitz also sat sheepishly avoiding McKenzie's eyes; instead, he glanced nervously at his wife. She showed no nervousness, no hesitation. This was her meeting, called at her insistence, and she meant to carry it through to its ruthless conclusion.

She nodded at Brackman, 'I'll take responsibility for this, Douglas.' Her voice was incisive, peremptory – a no-nonsense WASP lady laying down the law and not expecting to be contradicted: a voice that made Stuart Markowitz cringe in his seat.

Leland McKenzie sat down, staring gloomily at her over his bifocals and listening as she went on:

'We have a number of concerns, Leland, and we'd like to address them.'

'What kind of concerns?' – McKenzie's tone was flat, neutral.

'Concerns like leadership,' Ann Kelsey said. McKenzie raised an eyebrow but didn't reply. 'Specifically, your emerging track-record for deception. You have deliberately concealed your relationship with Rosalind Shays, while mandating that the rest of us support her.'

McKenzie raised a limp hand, 'Oh, please!' His face showed weary distaste.

But Ann Kelsey ploughed on, 'You secretly promised Grace she'd be head of litigation – without telling either me or Michael. Then just yesterday I found out you made a covert promise of a partnership to Jonathan, in exchange for his backing you against Rosalind.'

Both Michael Kuzak and Jonathan Rollins felt deeply uncomfortable at these revelations; but neither of them made any attempt to stem this venomous flow.

'My God, Leland!' she continued. 'Last week you sat in this room endorsing Jonathan here on his merits, when it was all really a political *payback*!'

McKenzie interrupted, 'I truly believe that Jonathan will make a great partner.' Although further down the table Jonathan Rollins didn't look so sure; the last thing he wanted was to have his candidacy for a partnership turned into a pawn in a dog-fight between the upright Ann Kelsey and Big Daddy McKenzie.

Becker came in now, laconic but remorseless, 'The point

is,' he told Leland, 'you don't make deals like that – and you, of all people, have got to know that.'

'And *today*,' Ann Kelsey joined in, 'I learn, through a little checking that Velnick Industries – our big new client for which we gave you all the credit – is in fact a subsidiary of the Tammon Group Corporation – a Corporation whose head lawyer *just happens* to be Rosalind Shays.' There was a mild intake of breath round the table. Ann Kelsey looked at each of them, then back to McKenzie, 'Did she refer this subsidiary to you?'

McKenzie's face was now the texture of dried putty. 'So what if she did?' he said, in a low growl.

'So *this*,' Kuzak broke in heatedly. 'So you didn't tell us – that's what, Leland! So since Rosalind's client controls us, she indirectly has some control over *us* here.'

'That's ridiculous,' said McKenzie.

'It's *not* ridiculous!' Markowitz piped up, gaining confidence with the growing unanimity round the table, as well as anxious to show support for his wife. 'You've completely subverted the democratic process here, Leland. You're running around making decisions that affect *all* of us – and you're keeping us in the dark.' He paused, nodding smugly, then sat back as though expecting a round of applause.

'You hired C.J. Lamb *unilaterally*,' Kuzak said brutally, not sparing his old mentor even further humiliation. 'And that decision, Leland – like all the others – should have been put to the vote. You hired Tommy Mullaney *unilaterally* – and that should have gone to a vote.' He paused, drawing in his breath, while Mullaney and C.J. Lamb both sat poker-faced, saying nothing.

McKenzie looked at Kuzak, as though about to say, '*Et tu, Brute?*' – then back to Ann Kelsey. 'I'm trying to build

21

the revenues back up,' he said at last, wearily. 'Trying to save the firm from the bankers. You know that –'

'Well, we don't like your methods,' Ann Kelsey snapped. 'We don't like the secrecy – *especially* now Rosalind Shays has got you eating out of her hand.'

McKenzie flushed, 'That's out of line, dammit!'

'Maybe so,' Markowitz said, quick to his wife's defence. 'But this is a partnership – not a dictatorship! And the purpose of this meeting is to have it all out in the open – to make our feelings clear.'

'Fine.' McKenzie nodded grimly. 'Now let me make *my* feelings clear. The burden is still on me to bring in the business. I can't spend eight hours a day trying to build a client-base, and also take time out to serve your sense of "democracy". Okay, I admit I may have been cutting some administrative corners, but I tell you – it's tough being both rainmaker and office ambassador at the same time.'

'So what are you saying?' asked Kuzak.

McKenzie looked at his young protégé with a pained expression, and said slowly, 'What I'm saying, Michael, is that I'm going to set my priorities. For the next six weeks I'm going to concentrate completely on expanding our client-list and free myself from all this bureaucracy.' He paused dramatically. The whole room went very quiet. 'I'm passing the Senior Partnership over to Douglas,' he said finally.

Brackman stared at him; opened his mouth to speak, then seemed to think the better of it and closed it again. It was Markowitz who spoke first, 'You can't do that!' he cried.

'I certainly can,' McKenzie replied, with a certain grim triumph. 'The Articles of Partnership authorise me to make a pro tem designation – *unilaterally* – and that's just what I'm doing.'

'But why him?' – Markowitz nodded rather desperately toward the solemn figure of Douglas Brackman at the head of the table – 'I mean,' he struggled, 'shouldn't we, um, kind of have a vote . . .?'

'Why him?' McKenzie repeated. 'I'll tell you why him. Because right now he's the only one I trust.'

He turned and looked at Brackman, sitting mute and slightly perplexed, at his side. 'Douglas, for the next six weeks you're in charge. I leave it to you to establish a fair democratic process that everyone can live with.' He stood up. 'Any more questions from anybody?' Silence. 'Good! Thank you for raising your concerns. This meeting is adjourned.'

With that, he turned on his heel and walked out. Behind him the silence was total. For a moment none of them even looked at each other. Leland McKenzie might not have won; but neither had anyone else.

*

Leonard Bey was already waiting in Becker's office when he entered. Becker nodded, 'Mr Bey! – what a surprise.' He sat down behind his desk and smiled at him. Bey did not smile back.

The big bronzed man appeared slightly shrunken: hunched in the client's seat, his deep tan looking dry and sallow in the refracted light from the half-drawn blinds. 'You don't know how this kills me,' he began, slowly, trying not to look directly at Becker through his dark glasses. His eyes behind them were deep-sunk, as though he'd not been sleeping well. His voice had a hoarse, defeated tone:

'Really kills me, Becker . . .' His large brown hand moved across the table and dropped a beige-coloured cheque in front of Becker. 'I would have sent it over by messenger but . . .' He frowned, then leant forward, peering earnestly at Becker through the smoky lenses, 'Listen – even though the deal says she can't talk about my . . . y'know' – he gave a vague, resigned gesture – 'well I know how lawyers tell war stories to each other and that . . . well, this would be a good one, I guess.'

'I won't tell anyone,' Becker said.

Leonard Bey seemed to relax a little. He sighed. 'I guess I must be the world's biggest sap, huh? Thinking that a girl like that could go for an old bore like me!'

'As much as I can tell about your ex-wife, Mr Bey,' – Becker shrugged dismissively – 'if I were you, I wouldn't bother measuring yourself by her standards.'

Bey gave a weak smile, 'But I do – you know that? Problem is, Becker, I grew up handsome. And I just can't face the reality that one day – if it isn't now – people are suddenly gonna think I'm not attractive any more. I'm gonna walk into a room, and girls like Christina just aren't gonna look.' He paused, took a deep breath, 'How old are you, Becker? Forty-two – forty-three?'

'Thirty-nine,' Becker said quickly.

'Yeah, well . . . Y'know what I mean. You still turning heads? That smile still work like it used to?'

Becker gave him the smile, but it was wry, downbeat. 'I don't really worry about it,' he said, just a little too casually. He knew too well what Bey meant.

'Yeah – well you're lucky then,' Bey said. 'Lucky you're

24

not vain. because ageing – there's nothing gradual about it, y'know. You're just suddenly *old*.'

Becker looked across at him with sudden sympathy; for a moment he almost liked the man. At the same time, he felt vaguely embarrassed. 'Is that why you got the implant?' he said.

Bey leaned even further forward: his jaw set, his eyes intense, even behind the shades. *Oh God*, thought Becker, *he's going to unburden himself now . . .*

'I didn't need it,' Bey said hoarsely. 'I wasn't impotent or anything. I just wanted to be as strong and as virile as . . . as I used to be.'

Becker shifted uncomfortably in his chair. 'Yeah . . .' – he glanced quickly at his watch – 'Look, Mr Bey, I'm sorry – but I do have an appointment.'

'Yeah,' Bey repeated gloomily. He sat for a moment studying his thumbs on the desk. 'Look,' he said suddenly, 'just tell Christina, will you, that I wish her all the best. Okay?'

'Okay,' Becker said. 'Sure I will.'

The big man got to his feet; seemed about to offer his hand to Becker; then changed his mind and walked wearily out of the room.

Becker just watched him; and then sat staring at the closed door. He felt he needed a drink: only it was far too early.

That damned Christina Sheppard was a real killer, he thought.

Chapter Four

The reception area of McKenzie Brackman and Partners looked like a quiet, old-fashioned nightclub. There were candles round the walls, stuck in old Italian wine bottles; one desk was lined with empty glasses and full bottles, spread on a white cloth; and there were clusters of coloured balloons on either side of the glass doors.

A procession of party guests came filing furtively out of the lifts. They gathered in the reception area like conspirators, talking in hushed whispers. Corrinne Becker came bustling up to the front and now stood bending over Roxanne's desk, which had been cleared of its word-processor, telephones and in and out trays; while in their place stood a large birthday cake encrusted with a thick layer of icing on which had been squeezed out, in a delicate pink scroll, the sugary message: *ARNIE – FROM ALL THE FIRM – ON YOUR 39th!*

Corrinne now began carefully lighting two rows of little white candles: three in the first row, above the inscription; nine in the second, underneath. It was all very tasteful, very decorative, and – at least in the opinion of Mrs Becker – altogether very touching. What was more, despite some

26

earlier misgivings, Corrinne remained confident that Arnie would find it so, too – when the time came. Poor Arnie, she thought, it always took time with him . . .

She made a last check to see all was well; while Roxanne was turning to the guests, raising her hands to her lips, '*Sh-shhhh . . .!* Everybody quiet, I'm going to get Arnie now . . .' And she began tiptoeing with exaggerated care towards the corridor and Arnie's office. She left behind her an unnatural quiet.

*

The evening was still young, not quite seven o'clock, and most of the firm would normally have gone home by then. But Arnie Becker was still in his office – Roxanne had already established that – and had been there since lunch, and wouldn't be going home till late. He was deeply immersed – as he'd told her, in some detail, earlier in the day – in a complicated wrangle between an ageing pop star called Madrigal 'C' (who'd been big in the Sixties and now made tawdry TV commercials) and his newest, very young wife, known aptly as 'Lolita' (who was the latest sizzling attraction on the Las Vegas circuit). She was suing her shop-worn husband after finding him in the matrimonial bed, happily snorting cocaine out of the navels of two naked bimbos he'd picked up on Venice Beach.

The police had not been involved – so far – and Becker, who'd been retained by Madrigal 'C', was having to work out a first line of defence against a possible drug rap. His problems were further complicated by the fact that his client had no money. Everything, it seemed – from the lavish mansion on Benedict Canyon to the pet Airedale terrier – belonged to Lolita. Becker knew he was going to have to go for the jugular, by trying to prove the wife had set up the whole thing, or risk seeing his client get a one-to-three for possession, plus a possible depravity charge, and have to pursue him to Sternville Open for his fee.

Then, in the middle of the afternoon – when Roxanne had called in on him with some papers – he'd told her that he'd just had a call back from the L.A.P.D. files, telling him Madrigal 'C' had a record for drug offences going back to before the Flood, and to cap it all, his client was still on a two-year probation.

Roxanne had seen that this latest piece of news had left him tense and worried. After relating the details, Becker had told her he must not be disturbed – he was going to have to work this out, even if it took him all night . . .

As she left him, she was worried too – knowing he'd hardly be in a congenial mood for the evening's surprise festivities. She knew how it would be by seven o'clock: Arnie's head would be aching; he'd have drunk too much black coffee, smoked too many cigarettes; and the only possible bonus, in his eyes, would be that the tortured affairs of Madrigal 'C' might have made him forget it was his birthday . . .

Roxanne was nervous as she approached his door, still on tiptoe. The corridor was dark, and very quiet. Then she noticed, with surprise, that there was no light showing under the door. She paused, holding her breath. Perhaps he was exhausted and taking a quick nap? It wouldn't be the first time she'd known Arnie assure everyone he was up to his ears in work and was not to be disturbed on any account – even to have phone calls put through – then quietly draw the blinds, remove his shoes, let back his hi-tech chair into the full reclining position and take a nice half-hour catnap while the rest of the firm went on working their butts off . . .

She was still holding her breath as she stepped furtively up to the door and knocked, very gently. There was no answer. She knocked again, harder. And for a moment she thought she heard something: a faint slithering, scuffling sound; then – *could it have been?* – a hurried whisper . . .

'Arnie?' she said, very softly. 'Arnie – you in there . . .? It's me – Roxanne!'

There was dead silence; then Becker's voice, barely recognisable, hoarse and urgent, 'Go away!'

She froze. *Oh God*, she thought. *He's ill – he's had a stroke* . . . And she had a horrible image of Arnie lying there on the carpet behind the desk, trying to drag his half-paralysed body across to the door, too stricken even to call for help . . . In a panic she tried the handle. It turned. She pushed the door open a couple of inches. '*Arnie . . .?*'

'Get out! Go away!' – louder this time, and closer, it seemed.

In desperation, Roxanne threw the door open and walked in. The room was in almost total darkness. There was another quick scuffling sound, like the one she thought she'd heard from outside; and two dim shapes began to materialise somewhere in front of her on the floor. She swung round and switched on the light.

'Arn . . .' she began; then stopped dead. In front of her, Arnie Becker was hopping on one leg, struggling to get his trousers on. He blinked into the sudden light, his eyes staring, his mouth wide-open, as if in a silent scream. Below him, clutching Becker's shirt across her breasts and shoulders, was Christina Sheppard. She was half-kneeling, her long naked legs straddled awkwardly across a pile of hastily discarded clothes.

Roxanne reacted with confusion and outrage. It wasn't that her beloved Arnie Becker was exactly behaving out of character – but the sight of him *in flagrante delicto* with a recent client, right here on the floor of his own office, offended even her robust, broad-minded sensibilities. Above all, she was horrified by the thought of what would happen if Corrinne were to find out.

Poor Corrinne Becker – who'd laboured so hard to make sure Arnie had a lovely surprise party for his birthday. Now all that was ruined.

'*Get up!*' Roxanne cried, in a furious whisper. '*Both of you!*'

'Are you crazy?' Becker's voice was almost as angry, but with an edge of desperation. '*Get out – !*'

'Shhhh . . .!'

'What the hell is the matter with you?' Becker cried hoarsely, getting his trousers up round his hips and reaching down for nis shirt.

'Your wife and twenty of your closest friends are out in reception, ready to throw you a surprise party! That's what's the matter with me!' Roxanne said, still whispering.

'Oh God,' Becker muttered.

'Get your clothes on! For God's sake – both of you!' – she paused, glanced hurriedly back out of the door, then added to Christina, 'Don't you go anywhere! You stay right in this office and you don't move until I come back and say you can!'

'Rox . . .' Becker began.

'Shut up and hurry, Arnie – or somebody's going to walk in – *you stupid jerk!*'

30

'Okay, okay . . .' He stood struggling with his shirt buttons, while beside him Christina Sheppard slipped into her clothes with the agility of a quick-change artiste. 'I'm ready . . .!' he panted, grabbing for his tie.

Roxanne stood in the doorway, shaking her head, and said out loud, 'Great time for a nap, Arnie!' – then whispered furiously, 'This is a surprise party – so you just look *surprised* dammit! You stupid, selfish, ungrateful pig!' She then turned and disappeared quickly back into the crowded reception area.

A moment later Becker came stumbling in, blinking at the sudden wall of faces, giving them all a glazed smile. One of the turn-ups of his trousers was caught in his sock, and a cuff-link was hanging loose.

He was met with a chorus of '*Surprise! Surprise!*' – which he acknowledged with a fatuous, agonised grin, boldly feigning surprise as he submitted to a loving kiss from Corrinne. He wondered bleakly, *Is there anything left in this world to surprise me?* as he broke away from her and looked round, exclaiming, 'Oh wow! This all for me . . .?'

At this, the whole assembly broke into a boisterous rendering of 'Happy Birthday to You!' – while Becker stood praying that the San Andreas Fault might choose this moment to yawn wide and swallow the whole of downtown Los Angeles into the burning vaults of the Earth.

But to give Arnie Becker full credit, he kept his face muscles so well disciplined, his smile so forced, so permanently rigid and glaring, that – of all these dear friends and colleagues and loved ones – only Roxanne could know that his apparent happiness was not genuine.

He swallowed three glasses of champagne, one after the

other, and for the moment forgot about Christina, or where she was, or how she was going to get out of there.

*

Some days later a much chastened Arnie Becker was at his desk, busying himself with a mass of case-work. He did not look up at first, as Roxanne strode in and dumped about half a ton of box-files and loose folders down in front of him. Some of them started to slide in a gathering avalanche towards the edge, and he was only able to grab them back after an ungainly lunge across the desk. When he straightened up, she was standing in front of him, hands on her hips, a smug smile on her plump, pretty face.

'Dammit, Roxanne! Enough is enough.'

She began to walk out, not even turning when he shouted, 'This has been going on for nearly a week. It's got to stop.' She paused, still smiling, but said nothing.

'I can't take any more of this hostility. Honest, Rox! I would think, under the circumstances, I'd get a little understanding.'

She turned then, measuring him with her calm, brown stare. 'The circumstances, Arnie, were that your wife was out there organising a surprise birthday party to show you how much she loves you – while *you* were in here' – she cast a disdainful glance at the floor, as though identifying the scene of some ghastly crime – 'committing sex acts with a client.'

'Exactly,' said Becker, facing her with an attempt at dignity. 'And have you any idea what it's like for me to cope with such guilt?'

'Oh, please!' She flinched slightly.

'Think about it, Roxanne. The easy thing to do would be to confess. To cleanse my conscience and unload my burden. But I don't. And you know why? Because it would hurt Corrinne too much – and I just couldn't bear to do that. So I hold it all in, suffering the pain myself – for her sake.'

Roxanne gaped at him, a look of sheer baffled wonderment and disbelief filling her whole face. 'You're incredible,' she murmured at last.

'Roxanne, I wasn't going to say this, but –' he paused, frowning miserably at the desk, 'and I don't want you to go worrying. But I'm sick. I am – I'm a sick man.'

'What do you mean – you're sick?'

'It's nothing to panic over yet. But I'm not well. I have what they call "satyriasis".'

'*Sata what?*'

'Satyriasis.' He went on looking down at the heap of files and documents in front of him. His face was drawn, pale. (*Perhaps he was sick, after all*, she thought.) He added, slowly, 'I don't even like to think about it myself. I'm just gonna go through whatever treatments I have to – live one day at a time. . . . And – and I'll beat this. I will. With the support of my family, and my friends. I know I'll beat it. Just be there for me, Rox. Give me strength.'

Roxanne just stood staring at him in pained disbelief. Poor Arnie, she thought. The trouble was, she'd thought of 'Poor Arnie' for so long now, there was no longer any novelty in it. Not even compassion. All she felt, to her horror, was mild contempt – and disgust.

*

33

Brackman looked down the conference table, dour and mildly aggressive, enjoying his newly acquired authority.

'All right – let's get started, people. First up – as Senior Partner, I've taken the liberty of setting up a few meetings with some of you this week, regarding various administrative matters.' His voice was dry and clipped; his eyes swivelling from one face to the next, penetrating yet impersonal.

'Stuart, you and I will meet after we've done here. Ann, I've got you slated for 2.15. Michael – 11.30 tomorrow, please.'

'I'm not sure I'm free,' Kuzak said.

'You are – I confirmed with your secretary. Jonathan, Tommy' – he nodded briskly at them both – 'I also have projects for you which we can discuss later.'

They were all glancing at each other now, disconcerted by this whirlwind of dogmatic efficiency; and they didn't like it. There were ways of doing these things – there was a McKenzie way, and now, it seemed, there was a Brackman way. Nobody said anything, Brackman continued.

'Moving on – Shaw versus Gendler.'

'That's mine,' said C.J. 'We represent the buyer of a house trying to rescind the sale. Trial starts today.'

'What grounds for the rescission?'

'It's haunted,' said C.J. simply.

'I beg your pardeon?' McKenzie said, from his new place half-way down the table.

'House is haunted,' C.J. said, with no more emphasis than if she were stating it had two garages. Somebody chuckled.

'Anything funny?' Brackman snapped.

'Nothing at all,' C.J. said. 'The buyers are taking it very

34

seriously. Two day trial at most. We should finish up by Friday.'

Brackman nodded. He looked impatient; the supernatural was not something he cared to get too involved in. He looked at Grace Van Owen, 'Grace – where does your court martial stand?'

'We go today.'

'What's the defence here?' asked Becker. 'I mean, the guy disobeyed a direct order during combat – what bigger form of treason can there be than that?'

'Refusing to attack innocent civilians doesn't spell treason to me,' Grace said, looking fiercely at him.

Becker shrugged; he was in no mood to get into verbal combat with Grace – at least, not so early in the day.

Brackman said, 'They weren't civilians – they were soldiers in the Panama Defence Force. They were guarding General Noriega.'

'You don't know that,' said Grace.

'I certainly know that General Noriega had to be captured,' Brackman expostulated, 'and if . . .'

'Not *that* way, he didn't,' said Ann Kelsey. 'Innocent people . . .'

'You had a better way, Ann?' Becker put in provocatively.

'It was a surgical strike,' Brackman said, frowning emphatically.

'Ah c'mon,' said Ann, 'We were just *looking* for an excuse to shatter the wimp image – that whole invasion was overkill!'

Becker groaned inwardly. *Here we go!* he thought. *The WASP liberal psyche at full throttle!* But Brackman cut in before he could speak, 'That's enough! You want to malign

35

the United States, you do it in your own time. Not during a staff meeting while *I'm* in the chair.'

Ann clenched her jaw and said nothing.

'We're adjourned,' said Brackman. He stood up, and without another glance at any of them, strode out of the room. The new King had been crowned. God save the King. Becker stretched and groaned. Another five weeks of this and he'd be ready for a long vacation in the Caribbean – and to hell with his new therapy courses. He didn't bother to share his feelings with the others; he knew they were shared already.

Chapter Five

Grace Van Owen met her client, Robert Braden, in a small office attached to the guardroom at Fort Ord, Southern California.

It was hot and stifling, with no fan, no air-conditioning: though the Lieutenant looked disconcertingly cool. He was a stiff, bullet-headed young man with curiously close-set eyes, giving the occasional appearance of having a squint. Grace – mindful of his youth, and of the charges against him – summed him up as headstrong, probably brave, and a bit of a prig.

He was accompanied by the Army's Defence Counsel, Captain Sam Danowitz, a studious-looking officer with glasses, who had already lost most of his hair before the age of forty. He said to Grace, in a solemn, meticulous voice, 'Kenners and Brumet definitely toe the Army line. Auerbach should be pretty sympathetic – but other than that, the panel's pretty stacked.'

'What about Colonel Messien?' she asked.

'Fair Judge,' said Danowitz thoughtfully, 'a fair draw. Rainero's one of their top Prosecutors, though. They always use him for their big ones.' He consulted his watch.

37

'I'll see what the hold-up is.' He nodded encouragingly at Braden, 'Hang in there, kid!'

Braden came instantly to attention, 'Yes, sir!' He waited till the Captain had left, then looked steadily at Grace. 'You'll be running the show in there – right, Ms Van Owen?' he said at last. He sounded surprisingly confident, even relaxed. 'No offence to Captain Danowitz,' he added hurriedly, 'I know he's on my side. But he's Army. And after all this is over, he still has to answer to these people.'

She nodded. 'Well, I don't. And you're going to get the best defence possible, Robert – I promise you that.'

'You think we can win?' he asked, with the first trace of anxiety.

She looked at him coolly. 'I don't know. They only need two thirds to convict. And this is a military court.'

A moment later Captain Danowitz reappeared. 'Okay. Ready to go?'

Braden came to attention again. Grace just nodded, 'Ready.'

*

The Courtroom had been set up at the end of a gymnasium. The floor was bare boards; the walls harsh brown, relieved by bleak expanses of hospital lime-green. The Stars and Stripes stood furled next to a steel climbing-frame, and a bronze eagle was perched on a ledge above the President's chair, on which Colonel Massien – a grave, jowly man with cropped grey hair – was seated, behind a table on a raised wooden platform. Below, sat the panel of seven Judges, all officers, ranking captain or above – a sombre group in immaculate dress uniform, who sat facing two tables and a row of uncomfortable steel chairs.

Grace Van Owen, Captain Danowitz, and their client, Lieutenant Braden, were at one table; and just behind them, an elderly couple, who sat watching the proceedings in a bewildered, dignified silence. These were Lieutenant Braden's parents.

At the adjacent table was the Army Prosecutor, Major Charles Rainero, a trim, dark man who looked as though he were nursing a successful career in the military and didn't intend to make any mistakes during this trial.

He had just called his first witness, Captain Paul Jaworski. A compact, sturdy man, with the look of a battle-hardened veteran, he stepped forward and took the oath. He had shrewd, careful eyes and the bearing of a soldier who could handle himself in a tight situation. He was telling the Court, 'The codename for the operation was "Urgent Fury". Our mission was to capture General Noriega and to bring him back to the United States for trial.'

'But specifically, sir,' Rainero asked, 'what were you trying to do on the night of December 20th, 1989?'

'I was in command of Alpha Company in the El Chorillo section of Panama City, where there were about a thousand troops loyal to General Noriega. My orders were to knock out their communications in three locations.'

'And how did you proceed, Captain?'

'I had deployed my men around the three buildings, when suddenly Lieutenant Braden's unit became pinned down by sniper fire. After discussing the situation with the Lieutenant' – Captain Jaworski gave a blank nod towards the accused – 'I ordered him to take out the snipers.'

'And were these orders carried out?'

'No – he refused. When I repeated the order, he again refused.'

'This was all while you were under enemy fire?'

Yes, sir. At that time I then gave the order to his platoon sergeant who carried the order out. The sniper fire was suppressed. After which I had Lieutenant Braden taken into immediate military custody, and I preferred charges for disobeying a direct order.'

'Thank you, sir.' Captain Rainero sat down, and his place was taken by Grace Van Owen. She looked very elegant in this stark military setting, but gave no sign of feeling out of place, still less of being intimated. She stood facing the tough Captain for a moment in calm silence.

'Captain Jaworski,' she said at last. 'Did Lieutenant Braden offer any reason for his behaviour?'

'Yes, ma'am. He claimed there were non-combatants positioned inside the building.'

'And where were *you*, sir, at this time?'

'At the C.P. – the Command Post, ma'am,' he added, for her benefit. 'Two blocks away.'

'So when Lieutenant Braden told you he saw civilians, you didn't know that to be false, did you?'

'Panamanian Defence Forces often dress up as civilians,' Jaworski answered simply. 'That means —'

This was a civilian neighbourhood, Captain,' Grace broke in. 'Are you telling this panel that there were no innocent people around?'

'I'm telling this panel,' the Captain replied doggedly, 'that there were *soldiers* entrenched in that neighbourhood – some of whom were spraying us with machine-gun fire.'

Grace nodded. 'So you started levelling buildings?' She paused. Captain Jaworski waited. 'May I remind you,

Captain, that the Geneva Convention specifically states that you have a duty to minimise civilian casualties? Is that not so?'

We have taken measures to ensure that the civilians left the area,' Jaworski replied obstinately.

'And what measures were those, Captain?'

Jaworski pursed his lips, 'Artillery support,' he said flatly.

'Artillery support,' she repeated, raising an eyebrow. 'That means you shelled them?'

'The bombardment was meant to discourage them from staying in the area.' The tough, weathered face was almost brutal in its impassivity.

'But we're talking about massive bombardment,' Grace said. 'Isn't it possible that people in there could have been too scared to move?'

'I have no idea,' Jaworski replied. He was showing signs of anger now.

'So you just went in with your tanks anyway?' Grace said, almost casually.

'My men were under fire, Counsellor.'

'Your men were under *sniper* fire, Captain. And you respond by ordering your tanks to destroy an entire civilian neighbourhood, where . . .'

'Hey, ma'am!' – Jaworski's lips were suddenly bloodless with anger – 'I'm the one who has to write the letters to the mothers and fathers, telling them their son is dead. *I'm* the one . . .'

'What about the Panamanian families?' Grace said. 'Who writes to *them*?'

Major Rainero was on his feet, 'Objection.'

41

The President, Colonel Massien, nodded at her, frowning, 'Counsel —'

She carried on. 'You give no warning to evacuate. You just start shelling their homes.'

'It was a war, lady!' For a moment Captain Jaworski was trembling.

'It wasn't a war until you attacked!' Grace said recklessly, raising her voice almost to a shout.

'You weren't there!' Jaworski shouted back, while Rainero intoned another 'Objection'.

Grace fixed Captain Jaworski with her level grey eyes. *'But Lieutenant Braden was there.* He was looking at the innocent people you ordered him to kill!'

Colonel Massien leant forward. 'Ms Van Owen, that's enough!'

She paused, her jaw stiff. 'I have nothing further,' she said, and sat down.

*

Second Lieutenant Robert Braden stood erect before the panel of seven Judges and answered Grace's questions like a catechism. 'We were pinned down for about ten minutes. There were about thirty of us on foot – maybe a hundred metres from the building. I was positioning my tank, when the order came.'

'The order being to take out the snipers?' said Grace.

'Yes, ma'am.'

'But Lieutenant . . . you refused to execute that order?'

'Yes, ma'am.'

'Could you tell the Court why?'

'Because as I was looking through my binoculars, I saw

many civilians in the area. All were unarmed. There were women and old people.'

'And what did they appear to be doing?'

'They appeared to be running for their lives.'

'Did any of them fire at you or your men?'

'No, ma'am.'

'Did you report this to Captain Jaworski?' said Grace.

'Yes. He just told me to carry out the order.'

'But you refused?'

'I would've killed too many innocent people. I just couldn't do that,' Braden said.

'Thank you, Lieutenant,' said Grace; and returned to her seat.

*

Major Charles Rainero, the Army Prosecutor, now rose to face the accused officer. 'Your men were under machine-gun fire, were they not?'

'In my opinion, there were many more civilians than there were snipers,' Braden replied.

'*In your opinion.*' Rainera made no effort to conceal the bitter irony in his voice. 'As part of your training in preparation for the invasion of Panama City, you were told that the Panamanian solders often dressed up like civilians. That's not an opinion. That's a *fact* – is it not?'

'Yes.' Braden still stood erect, his face impassive.

'And yet here you are – in combat – suddenly deciding which is which.' Rainero's voice was as sharp and precise as a dentist's drill.

'I know what I saw,' Braden replied staunchly. 'Those people weren't soldiers.'

43

'Well,' said Major Rainero, 'why don't you describe the distinctions for us, Lieutenant?' He gestured with his arm towards the panel of Judges. 'Why don't you tell these majors and captains here the secret – because you seem to be the only expert here.'

'I *saw* them,' Braden said. 'Soldiers don't run around scared like that.'

'You disobeyed a direct order from your Commanding Officer because of the way these people were *running around*? Is that it?'

'They were in a panic,' Braden said, his voice breaking for the first time.

'Is it possible,' Rainero said, pressing home his advantage, 'that these were PDF soldiers in a panic in the face of overwhelming fire-power?'

'I didn't believe that to be the case.'

'You didn't *believe* that to be case?' – Major Rainero let his contempt seep into every syllable, every facial movement – 'And so, based on a hunch, you decided to disobey a direct order.'

'These people were —' Braden began; but Rainero snapped back before he could finish:

'Answer the question! Isn't that what happened?'

'Yes.' For the first time Braden's voice was subdued, his head slightly lowered.

'Thank you, Lieutenant. That's all.' Major Rainero did not look at the accused as he sat down. He was like a man who had just performed a particularly unpleasant task, which he considered beneath his dignity, and he wanted it over as quickly as possible.

On the benches behind, Lieutenant Braden's parents sat,

old and worried and bowed. They loved their son and they feared for him.

*

Corrinne Becker came hurrying into the office complex, looking harassed – trying to keep her dignity, to keep calm and cheerful, as she headed straight for Roxanne's desk.

Roxanne was getting used to these visits by Mrs Becker. Since Arnie's surprise party all her female instincts made her sympathetic to the woman's plight. But, whereas the early visits had been occasional – at first, even a pleasant surprise, because everyone liked Corrinne and was glad to see her – recently her appearance in the office had become more regular, even persistent. As usual, Roxanne looked up smiling, as Corrinne approached.

'Hi Rox!'

'Hi,' Roxanne said. 'Arnie's in Probate all afternoon, Corrinne. I'm not even sure he's coming back to the office today.'

'I know' – Corrinne had dropped her smile, as she leant closer to Roxanne, lowering her voice – 'I came to talk to you, Rox. In private.'

Roxanne nodded, frowning slightly. 'Okay.' She began to stand up. 'We can go into Arnie's office.'

'Is that safe?' Corrinne said: 'I mean, he's not likely to come back suddenly?'

'No, I promise. He's out all day.' Roxanne led the way out of the complex, over to Becker's unlocked door. Corrinne followed, looking faintly nervous. When they were inside, Roxanne closed the door and stood with her back to it. 'What's up, Corrinne?'

The woman took her time, seating herself tentatively in the client's chair in front of her husband's desk. 'I think Arnie's having an affair,' she said at last.

'Excuse me?' Roxanne's surprise was feigned, of course, but not entirely false: what took her aback was the directness of Mrs Becker's approach.

'Roxanne, I don't mean to put you in the middle – and if I am, I'm sorry. I know how far back you go with Arnie and . . .' She watched Roxanne walk over behind the desk and sit down in Becker's chair. '. . . It's just that I'm feeling a little desperate.'

'About what?' Roxanne was suddenly very uncomfortable, fearing the worst.

'There's something wrong,' Corrinne said. 'I can just feel it with him – for the last week he's been completely solicitous. Like he's feeling guilty. I know it's unfair of me to come to you like this.' She paused, looking beseechingly across at Roxanne, her lips beginning to quiver. 'Is . . . is he having an affair?'

'Not to my knowledge – no.' Roxanne's voice seemed to come from somewhere far way, outside her: for her country upbringing had taught her that to tell a naked lie, with intent, was most surely inviting misfortune.

'So – I'm just being paranoid?' The woman's face was pale, crumpled, desperate. 'Is that it? Nothing's happened?' A small pathetic gleam of hope appeared in her dark eyes. 'I'm just being paranoid – yes?'

Roxanne said nothing; she felt as though she'd been turned to stone.

'Rox? Please. Is that it?'

When Roxanne finally forced herself to speak, her voice still seemed unnaturally far away – only this time she wasn't lying through her teeth. 'I don't think it's appropriate for me to talk about . . .' – her words dropped like stones into a well – 'about Arnie's personal life.'

Corrinne Becker sat staring at her for a long moment. Roxanne's lie had been wasted, was now dead: and in that moment Corrinne knew everything. 'Oh, my God,' she said quietly.

Roxanne said nothing. The girl in front of her began trembling slightly, all over, but she preserved her dignity. She stood up, her eyes still dry, and turned quickly towards the door.

At the last moment, Roxanne cried, 'Corrinne!' But she was too late. Mrs Becker was outside and the door closed firmly behind her.

Roxanne sat aghast, horrified at her own callousness. What had she done? What could she do now? She'd have done better to have stuck to the lie. And to have gone on lying . . .

Chapter Six

In front of the court martial stood a firm-jawed, worldly-looking woman in her late thirties: her blonde hair scraped back in a functional bun, her dress smart but casual, as she eyed Grace Van Owen with a hard, cynical, I've-seen-it-all-and-so-what-expression.

'Yes, I've been a journalist with the *Miami Tribune* for the last seven years.' She sounded almost bored.

'And you have been assigned to Panama City, Ms Dawson?' Grace asked.

'Yes. Specifically to investigate General Noriega's involvement with Miami drug-trafficking.'

Major Rainero rose to his feet. 'Your Honour – I renew my objection to this witness. She has no relevance to . . .'

'She was there the night of the invasion,' Grace snapped.

Colonel Massien nodded. 'Then let's just get to that part, shall we?' he said politely.

'Ms Dawson,' Grace went on, 'could you tell us what transpired the night of December 20th 1989?'

'Yes. I was interviewing one of my sources in El Chorillo. Suddenly the whole sky lit up with fire – explosions from American gunfire.'

'Did you have any idea this was coming?' Grace asked.

'None. I was caught in the middle of it, like everybody else.'

'What did you do, Ms Dawson?'

'Well, we made it to a Catholic church. It was the only brick building around and people knew it wouldn't burn. The rest of the town was just gutted.'

'What did you see that night?' asked Grace.

'Mostly, I saw American military and American tanks. I saw members of the Panama Defence Force fighting back. I saw people running for safety – running for their lives.'

'There were civilians in the area?' said Grace.

'This was a residential area, Counsellor. People lived there.'

'And were civilians killed?'

'Sure they were. A lot of them were killed. Thousands more were injured. The gentleman I interviewed that night – he was killed. He was a civilian.'

'After that night, when did you next see this man?'

'Two weeks later – when I identified his body. He'd been dug up from a mass grave.

'Objection,' said Rainero.

'Your Honour,' said Grace, 'I ask . . .'

'This isn't just irrelevant,' Rainero said, 'it's prejudicial, and . . .'

Grace rounded on him, tense with anger, 'You have to let me put on a defence! I can't bring up witnesses all the way from Panama – and this witness *was there*! You . . .'

Colonel Massien sighed, 'All right, Ms Van Owen, I'll allow you some latitude, but I reserve my ruling on the admissibility of the testimony.'

Grace nodded and turned again to the witness, 'What do

49

you mean, Ms Dawson, when you said his body was dug up?'

'There was more and more information . . .' – the woman gave a vague, sardonic gesture – 'information that the dead civilians had been collected up by American troops and buried in mass graves, to cover up the fact that innocent lives had been lost.' She paused. 'One of these mass graves was found.'

'By who?' said Grace.

'By relatives of the dead. People looking for their lost family members.' The woman journalist's bland delivery made the meaning of her words all the more shocking. 'They found a hundred and twenty-three rotting bodies in the Jardin de Paz Cemetery – stuffed into plastic bags.'

'Who put them there?'

'The U.S. Army admitted doing it,' the woman said. 'No identification. No notification to the families. Our military killed innocent civilians, then stuffed them into garbage bags.'

Throughout this, Major Rainero sat grimly making notes. He didn't look at the witness once.

Grace went on, 'How many civilian casualties resulted from the United States invasion of Panama, Ms Dawson?'

'Three hundred have been confirmed dead. Some reports put the real figure at twice that. We'll probably never know.'

'Why is that?'

'In my opinion' – the woman paused only a fraction of a second – 'because the Army engaged in a massive cover-up. They killed a lot of innocent people. They trampled down an entire town and left fifteen thousand homeless. And they don't want the people back here to know about that.'

50

'Thank you, Ms Dawson. I have nothing further.'

Grace returned to her seat and Major Rainero stopped writing. He slowly stood up.

'Ms Dawson,' he began, 'do you have any knowledge that our military was trying to kill civilians?'

'No – and I don't believe they were. They were going after General Noriega's men.'

'That's correct,' Rainero said. 'And did you ever see an American soldier directly shoot a civilian?'

'Directly at them?' – again the woman hesitated only a moment – 'No. But in all the fires and explosions . . .'

Major Rainero gave her a little bow, 'Thank you, ma'am. And to your knowledge, it's possible that Panamanian Defence Forces *did* occupy the building that Lieutenant Braden was ordered to target? Right?'

'That's certainly possible. But . . .'

'And ma'am' – Rainero gave her another little bow – 'just so I'm clear on *your* disposition here' – he hesitated, with a cunning smile – 'you've written various articles *prior to this event*, which were extremely critical of the United States military presence in Panama – right?'

The woman stiffened, as though having her professional integrity challenged by a soldier was the basest affront imaginable. 'Yes, that's right,' she said proudly.

Major Rainero allowed a short silence to hang in the air – knowing the panel of Judges was deeply, if unconsciously, prejudiced against people who made their living attacking the military – before nodding briefly to the witness. 'Thank you, Ms Dawson. That's all I have.' As he returned to his chair, the Major guessed that this last exchange had probably just tipped the balance.

51

*

It was late and Becker was tired. Dead, dog-tired. He was worried about his health – physical, as well as mental. For recently he'd taken to considering himself, in an excess of self-pity bordering on paranoia, as variously a cripple, a mental wreck, a psychopath, even a pervert.

He drove home, through the darkened suburbs, like an automaton – so exhausted that when he got home he hadn't even the energy to nose the car into the garage.

He had begun to let himself in, pushing the door open, when he noticed that something was wrong. The light was off, and he stepped forward and stumbled over a pile of suitcases. Several of them were draped with clothes – suits, ties, shirts . . . It took him a moment to realise they were *his* clothes. All piled in a heap, without even being packed.

He groped for the light, turned it on – and only then did he see Corrinne standing at the foot of the stairs, waiting for him.

He blinked at her. 'What the hell is this?'

She was very pale, her eyes dark and hollow with recent weeping. It was a moment before he realised that she was also very angry.

'This is you moving out – that's what this is,' she said, in a flat, toneless voice.

He stared at her. *Had she been waiting all this time, in the dark, just to tell him that?* he thought wildly, at first too stunned to take it all in. 'Corrinne? I don't – I . . .'

'You're sleeping around, Arnie Becker. As a result, this marriage is over.'

'Hold on a second.' He felt the slender, cold fingers of panic gripping at his throat.

Her next words knocked him back as though he'd been punched:

'You have no idea how much you disgust me.' Her neat, pretty features were suddenly distended; the nostrils of the tilted nose flared – a horrible, frightening apparition of rage, of malice, of the female scorned and ready to strike back without mercy.

But his wits hadn't quite deserted him yet. 'I'm only disgusted with *myself*,' he said, his voice sliding into self-pity.

'I don't know what you're talking about!' she cried, as though unable to endure the sound of his voice any more. 'My God – are you going to start telling more lies? Or are you just one of those white-collar psychopaths who can't *help* telling lies, even when you don't have to? Or maybe you're just stupid? *Dumb!* A stupid, dumb divorce lawyer with nice blue eyes and a fancy smile. Passed your Law exams and that's that! That's all it takes for integrity, honesty, plain-dealing . . . *sanity* . . .'

Becker shuddered at the mention of that word, but couldn't manage to break in – perhaps too stunned, too utterly shocked by her fury even to open his mouth.

She was now almost hysterical with rage and misery, 'Does Arnie Becker – the *great*, the *wonderful*, the *lovable* Arnie Becker – think he can just go on spinning lies and more lies, until . . .'

'Corrinne!' he tried to reach out, to grab her, control her – vaguely worried now that if she carried on like this, she might in some way injure herself.

But she flinched away. 'Don't touch me! You make me sick!'

He recoiled, groaning inwardly: Oh God! How many

times had he heard clients describing exactly this scene, even repeating these exact lines of dialogue, word for word: *'Don't touch me! . . . You make me sick . . .!'*

But this was for real. It wasn't something he could detach himself from; listening with feigned compassion while the lawyer's taxi-meter ticked away, at four hundred dollars per hour . . .

He said desperately, 'Corrinne – please – it was a one-time thing . . .!' But they were the wrong words. They were the spring, the fuse, the straw that broke the camel's back. His wife went berserk. She began flailing her little fists at him, screaming, 'You shut up! You just shut up! You pig! My God, you filthy pig! How I hate you!'

Suddenly, in a kind of static horror, she turned. At the foot of the stairs stood a small child, her eyes wide with uncomprehending terror. Corrinne drew in her breath, momentarily reining herself in. 'Chloe – go to bed, honey,' she called softly.

'Why are you crying?' the child said, with that strange all-seeing innocence of the very young.

Corrinne had taken her round the shoulder, and was already steering her towards the stairs. 'Go back to bed. Please, honey. I'll be there in a minute – just go back to bed right now . . .'

Becker stood rigid, numb, staring. The child glanced at him, then at her mother, and then turned and began walking slowly up the stairs. Corrinne waited till the last second: when the child was out of sight she sank her face in her hands.

'Oh God, what have I done to her . . .? I let her get attached to you – I let her love you . . . Oh God.'

'Corrinne . . . please let me explain' – his voice was hoarse, broken, pleading.

'No, Arnie. Get out. Just *get out*! Now.'

Chapter Seven

In the brown–green drabness of the makeshift Courtroom Grace Van Owen had risen to give her closing argument in defence of Second Lieutenant Robert Braden, on the charge of treason.

'Everybody in this country,' she said, 'everybody *everywhere* wanted to get General Noriega.' She paused, knowing it was going to be a hard run, against hard odds. They hadn't liked what she'd said before about the military killing civilians. And they hadn't liked the Dawson woman either – a mere journalist, a well-paid voyeur with a job to stiff the military: retelling a good story, with a nasty frill, about mass graves and unmarked garbage sacks being used for body-bags. That sort of ugly crap made good evening sound-bytes but it had nothing to do with real soldiering under fire; making hard decisions in the fog of war . . . even if the story were true.

Grace was going to have to win round those seven hard men in uniform, or lose the case and send Second Lieutenant Braden to the stockade for several, maybe many, years of his life.

'General Noriega was crushing democracy in Panama,'

she went on. 'He was running drugs into the United States – and he seemed to be laughing at America all the way to the bank. And when we invaded Panama, just over a year ago, and finally flushed him out . . . well' – she gave a sad, ironic gesture – 'we all cheered.'

No-one in the gymnasium at Fort Ord cheered. No-one moved. Besides the two M.P.s by the door, Grace was the only one standing – a small lone figure, in a trim blue suit and white blouse.

'Oh yes, we all cheered. At first. But then later, some of the cheering stopped, when it became clear exactly what our military had done. In violation of the Geneva Convention, we deliberately disregarded the safety of innocent people – we used overwhelming fire-power to flatten a civilian neighbourhood. Killing women and children . . . making fifteen thousand people homeless. . . .' Her words fell into a deep, leaden stillness.

'We didn't warn anybody. We just went on blasting.' She paused, and turned slowly towards the accused, sitting stiff and immobile next to Captain Danowitz. 'But Lieutenant Braden did not go on blasting away. He couldn't – just *couldn't* – even though he certainly knew that he'd be court-martialled if he violated military command. But he also had the plain guts to know – yes, *guts*, gentlemen! – to know that by *following* orders, he'd be carrying out morally reprehensible acts, as well as violating International Humanitarian Law – a Law that requires all armies to protect civilians whenever possible.'

She paused again, swallowed to moisten her throat, then continued, quietly, 'I know I'm not Army. You gentlemen probably look and me and think, "How can she possibly understanding the military?" And maybe I don't. But my father was in World War Two – he was shot at in anger, many times. And I grew up listening to his stories . . . and feeling his pride at having risked his life to protect the values this great country stands for.' She paused again, lowered her eyes for a moment, as though to honour her dead father, then raised them again, looked straight at Lieutenant Braden, then at the panel of Judges. 'I've always believed – and I still *do* believe – that we're the good guys. But I'm not sure we were the good guys that night in Panama. And c'mon, gentlemen – let's not pretend I'm the only one in this room with doubts.

'That night Lieutenant Braden turned to his conscience. For his sake, right now, I'm asking you to turn to yours.' She fixed her grey eyes on the seven uniformed men who sat watching her, mute as statues; then returned slowly to her seat.

*

Major Rainero now rose. He seemed tense; he was also angry, determined that the attempts by two aggressive, over-confident women civilians to cast calumnies on the honour of the U.S. military should not be allowed to triumph. There was more at stake here, in this grubby Courtroom, than the liberty of one high-minded junior officer who considered a brief experience in combat to be above the collective wisdom of his superiors. At least, that was how Major Rainero interpreted it, as he now braced himself for his closing argument:

'The Geneva Convention does not apply here,' he began. 'I am telling you, as a statement of fact – incontrovertible fact – that Panamanian soldiers were present in that building, making it a legitimate military target. Of course, it was a tough call – but Captain Jaworski *made* the call . . . and Lieutenant Braden wilfully disregarded it. He disregarded it. Disregarded it *while in combat* – while his own men were *under enemy fire*.' He paused for effect. He needn't have done. Colonel Massien and his colleagues did not actually nod their agreement, but their expressions said as much.

'Here, I should remind you' – Rainero looked directly at Grace this time, as though his next words were of no interest to the panel of Judges – 'remind you, ma'am, that a military – *any* military – has to have discipline where the chain of command is instantly honoured. *Without question*. The moment it's *not* honoured – the moment junior officers are entitled to call the shots, or say, 'This order I will obey – that one I won't' – then we won't have much of an Army, will we? We'll have a lot of opinion, a lot of chaos, and a lot of dead soldiers.'

He paused, his eyes still fixed on Grace. Behind him, Braden's parents were also looking at her – seeking, perhaps, some sign, some chance expression on her face that would give them hope; some inkling that the military were not all as hard and dogmatic as this cruel prosecuting Major. But Grace's face was grave, impassive, and gave no sign, no hope, as she sat listening to Rainero's relentless monologue:

'We put eighteen and nineteen-year-olds into combat with massive weapons. Now' – he gave a broad, ironic shrug – 'we can have them in the middle of battle, weighing up in their minds the merits of International Law, and pondering their own various interpretations of the Geneva Convention . . . or we can have them just following orders. Not a

59

tough choice, gentlemen.' This time Rainero addressed Colonel Massien and the seven Judges. 'You just have to decide whether you want us to *win* wars – or *lose* them.'

The eight officers sat looking at Captain Rainero. Not one of them spared even a glance for Lieutenant Braden. *A bad sign*, thought Grace. It wasn't, perhaps, infallible: but she'd never known a jury who looked away from a defendant after the closing arguments, and then went on to acquit.

*

'Members of the panel, have you reached your verdict?'

'We have, your Honour. Under Article 133 of the Uniform Code of Military Justice (conduct unbecoming an officer) including Article 90 (disobeying an order from a senior commander) and Article 99 (misbehaviour before the enemy) ... we find the Defendant, Robert Braden, guilty of all charges.'

Colonel Massien nodded gravely. 'Anything on sentencing, Major?'

Major Rainero rose. 'We'll be seeking thirty years, maximum security, your Honour.'

The Colonel looked down at Grace. 'Ms Van Owen?'

Grace rose slowly, glancing briefly over her shoulder at Mrs Braden; the woman was weeping quietly. Beside her, her husband sat absolutely still, as though dazed or drugged.

Grace said, 'Your Honour, before sentencing, I'd like the panel to hear from Lieutenant Braden.'

Braden glanced at her for a moment; then nodded and stood up. 'Sir' – his voice was calm but obviously unrehearsed, his broken sentences only adding to the conviction of what he was saying – 'I went into ROTC at school 'cause it helped pay my tuition fees. I knew it meant I had a debt to my country . . . and that maybe I'd even have to go to war some day and die for my country. And I was prepared to do that. I am still prepared to give my life for my commanding officers – or for the men who serve under me.' He paused, leaning forward slightly, his hands clasped tightly together in front of him. His face was very white, though his voice remained steady:

'I was ordered to blow up innocent people. To take out sniper fire, I was ordered to destroy a civilian building. I said no to that. Under the same circumstances, I'd say no again. No matter what my Government is try to prove.' And he sat down.

Amen to that, thought Grace. She smiled wearily at the young man, squeezed his mother's arm, and waited.

*

Arnie Becker stood in his office, red-faced, his hair awry, his suit rumpled, his breath coming in quick gulps so that his usually mellifluous voice was broken by angry splutters.

In front of him, Roxanne waited with hands folded, looking nervous but defiant. She thought she knew Arnie well enough by now to deal with all his moods and tantrums; but this was different. This was serious. She'd never seen him so angry.

'You betrayed me!' he said, in a little rasping croak. '*You goddam went and betrayed me!*'

'She suspected you were having an affair and . . .'

'And you confirmed it!'

'All I did was refuse to lie,' she said helplessly. 'It was an impossible situation!'

'Yeah' – he was suddenly pale now, his pursed lips curling into an uncharacteristic snarl – 'well, you won't ever have to face it again. You're fired.'

'*What?*'

'Nobody – *nobody* – does to me what you just did! You ruined my life!'

Roxanne's face suddenly crumpled. Her eyes swam, her voice quivered. 'You did this to yourself, Arnie! Can't you at least recognise the fact that . . .'

'I said you're fired! I don't want to hear anything else from you! Just pack up your crap and get the hell out of here.'

For a moment she just stood there, gaping helplessly at him. She was too angry, too shocked even to break down and cry. Finally, with enormous effort, she turned on her heel and walked out.

Becker balled a fist and drove it, with ferocious force, into the open palm of his hand. It hurt. *The bitch*, he thought: the stupid, self-righteous, stuck-up little humbug of a bitch. He smoothed his hair, straightened his jacket and marched out after her.

*

The door to Arnie Becker's office was half-open. Perhaps Roxanne had forgotten to close it: or perhaps she half wanted someone to witness her humiliation at the hands of the fickle and perfidious Arnie Becker. It was so typical of the man to blame those nearest him for his present troubles.

She was bent almost double, scooping the last of her files,

62

letters, documents, a few personal trifles like combs and scent and cologne sachets into a big plastic bag, when Douglas Brackman came strolling past. He glanced inquisitively through the door, frowned, and stepped inside.

'Rox – what are you doing?'

'Arnie fired me.' She spoke without looking up, determined to preserve some dignity.

'Why?' Brackman's frown deepened. '*Why?*' he repeated.

She straightened up, her eyes bright and dry. 'It's not important. I'm just not working here any more, that's all.' And she resumed her task, dropping a handful of address cards and blank memo forms into the bag.

There was a deep pause. 'Would you like to work for me?' Brackman said suddenly.

She stood up again, blushing this time. 'Well, gee . . . that's mighty nice of you, Douglas. But . . .'

'I'll raise you a hundred and twenty-five dollars a week – effective now,' he said.

She blushed deeper. 'That breaks the secretarial cap.' She gulped with emotion. 'I'm already in the top tier – why would . . .?'

'You wouldn't be a secretary,' Brackman said sharply. 'I need an assistant to help me with office management. I'm talking about a big promotion, Roxanne.'

She looked at him incredulously.

'More power, more money,' he went on. 'If you find me too impossible to work for, you just quit. What's not to try?'

Roxanne just stood there, not knowing whether to cry with joy or grief. Then, for a dangerous moment, she thought of throwing her arms round Douglas Brackman's neck and kissing him smack in the middle of his bald dome.

But she resisted the temptation. Instead, she looked at him
and smiled.

Chapter Eight

It was a nice house. Arnie and Corrinne Becker had only
had it for seven months: they'd snapped it up as a bargain,
in the recession, determined not to worry about the colossal
loan repayments until later – if at all. They could afford
them, after all, on their joint incomes – and anyway, what
was a mere loan to get in the way of true married bliss?

Yes, it was a nice house. Where the Ocean breezes
whispered up through the eucalyptuses on Westwood
Canyon, usually clearing the smog by lunchtime. And by
evening it was always cool: the only noise, from cicadas and
the gentle swish of lawn sprinklers. A dream house, outside
a dream city. L.A. – City of Angels.

*

Arnie Becker leaned against the push-bell under the white
porch. He heard it ring inside. There were dark rings under
his eyes, which were about the same colour as the setting
sun behind him. He looked as though he hadn't slept more
than a couple of hours a night for weeks. He looked ill.

The door opened. Corrinne was standing there, her dark

hair catching a halo of gold from the last of the sun. Becker straightened up; his voice was a little hoarse. 'Hi. Thanks for agreeing to see me.'

She looked at him without moving. 'What do you want to say?'

'That I'm sorry. That what I did was unforgivable. It happened *once* – the only time it's ever happened since we've been married . . .' He almost choked on the words, terrified he was going to start sobbing. 'Not that that makes it any less excusable but . . . but there's no trend here, Corrinne – I promise you!' It seemed to be getting darker even as he spoke: and all he could see were his wife's large, beautiful dark eyes staring back at him. They seemed to have no expression, beyond their beauty.

'And I also wanted to say,' he went on, 'that I can't picture my life without you and Chloe. I'll do anything to fix this, Corrinne!'

She could see he meant it – could see he was a broken husk of a man, pleading for what he'd once had and was not about to lose. A selfish, greedy, stupid bastard of a husband who thought he could have it all ways, and to hell with everyone who really mattered.

And now he came here whimpering on her doorstep, begging to be forgiven, to be allowed back in. Like a big, stupid, snivelling schoolboy who's been caught out and can't take his punishment . . .

'I've hired a lawyer,' she said flatly. 'The divorce papers will be filed probably by the end of next week.'

'You don't think that's a little rash?' He tried to sound calm suddenly, professional – but the sob was swelling like a stone in his throat.

66

'Marrying you was rash,' she answered, still not moving from inside the door.

'C'mon, Corrinne' – his tone half pleading, half aggressive – 'this was one stupid slip. It doesn't . . .'

'That's who you are – that's what you are. I feared it when we went into this, Arnie – and so did *you*.' She paused, her eyes blazing in the dying sun. 'If I weren't a parent, it might've been okay to take one more chance on you. But to be so reckless with my daughter's life . . .' – she broke off, with a shudder – 'I'm certainly not going to make that mistake again.'

A grip of terror now seized him. 'Oh God! Give me another chance, Corrinne. Please!'

'I'm following the advice of one of my former lawyers – a very *good* lawyer. "*Walk away from the problem – get on with your life.*"' She put her hand in the pocket of her slacks and handed him a card, 'This is my *new* attorney. From now on, you *don't* call me.'

She stepped back and quietly closed the door. Becker was left feeling like a man who's just been hit on the back of the neck, then kicked in the groin. His knees wobbled, his stomach felt like cold jelly; and for a moment he nearly vomited. Instead, he leant against the plaster colonnade of the porch and began to cry.

*

Colonel Massien cleared his throat and prepared to pass sentence.

'Lieutenant Braden, we have a great deal of sympathy for you. Your record indicates that you're an outstanding man and a fine officer. And we don't think any twenty-two-year-

67

old can ever be fully prepared for that first time he goes into combat.'

He paused, clearly his throat again. 'There are also some very serious questions about our military's actions in Panama. We gave no warning before we attacked. With ten Panamanian civilian deaths for every *one* American military death, it's unlikely that we really did try hard enough to minimise civilian casualties, as we're required to do under the Geneva Convention.

'Gathering up the civilian corpses and dumping them into mass graves in garbage bags, without even notifying the families ... well, it's true, that's a disgrace, pure and simple. And as soldiers and officers, we should be both shocked and embarrassed.' He paused; slowly, solemnly shaking his head, like some elderly senator running for re-election, and trying to be everyone's good guy; seeing all sides of the problem.

Grace thought sourly, *The Guy's just a little too good to be true*. For these fine, liberal sentiments from the Court President were, she was sure, just so much sugaring of what was going to be a very bitter pill.

Colonial Massien went on, 'But of all the sins committed that night, Lieutenant, the most dangerous – and potentially the most far-reaching – was *yours*. You disobeyed a direct order during combat. For soldiers wilfully to disregard superior officers while under enemy fire ...' – he raised one hand, then let it fall, in a dismissive chopping motion – 'there can be few greater threats to our national security. Accordingly, it was the sentence of this panel that you be confined at hard labour, for a period of ten years – to be served at the U.S. Disciplinary Barracks, Fort Leavenworth, Kansas.'

In the bleak silence, Braden's mother began to weep again.

*

'I'm not giving up, Robert. The appeal will be filed tomorrow – we're not giving up,' she repeated. Grace's eyes were shadowed with tiredness and despondency.

Braden nodded. 'Yeah – thanks,' he said simply. 'Thanks for everything, Ms Van Owen.'

There was a clatter outside; boots slammed on concrete; and Major Rainero came in, flanked by two white-helmeted military police.

'Lieutenant,' Rainero said, as the two M.P.s sprang to attention.

Braden sprang up also. 'Major!'

'I'm sorry about the sentence, Lieutenant. I think what you did was wrong, but . . .' – Rainero paused, his voice firm but gentle – 'I also think that with three hundred thousand soldiers in the Persian Gulf . . . well, the panel had to make an example of you.'

'Will you go on record with that, Major?' Grace said, standing up too.

'It's only an opinion, Counsel,' Rainero said, barely glancing at her.

Thanks for nothing, she thought, remembering something her old papa used to say: *Opinions are like assholes – we all got 'em!*.

'Let's go,' said one of the M.P.s. He placed a white gloved hand on Braden's sleeve.

Braden turned and hugged his mother, whose sobs now

69

came in loud, deep gasping sounds; then turned and shook his father's hand, and at the last moment hugged him too.

'Good luck, son,' the old man muttered.

Braden looked at them both for one last time. Then stood to attention again and said, 'Okay,' to the two M.P.s. As he passed Rainero, he saluted smartly, and Rainero saluted back.

Grace found herself strangely, deeply moved.

*

Tom Baker, a big rugged man in his late fifties, wasn't beating about the bush. He sat across the desk from McKenzie and said, 'I think I'm losing Feldcore, Leland.'

McKenzie was more than surprised: he was aghast. '*What?*' he cried.

Feldcore was an industrial conglomerate that stretched from the West Coast up into Canada and down to Central America. It dealt in 'commodities': chemicals, agricultural products, household goods, stationery – anything from explosives to ballpoint pens. Its annual turnover was more than the G.N.P. of most medium Third World countries, and McKenzie Brackman and Partners had a slice of the action. Leland McKenzie was one of the corporate lawyers for their Californian branch.

The man in the client's chair nodded grimly. 'Steven Wendle – the Senior Vice-President. He's been leading a back-stabbing campaign to push me out as Chief Executive Officer. My moles tell me he could succeed.' Although the room was cool, the big man was sweating profusely. He dragged a big silk handkerchief out of his breast pocket and began to wipe his neck and forehead with it.

'That can't be right,' Leland said lamely: he was almost too shocked and dismayed to think straight, for Baker's news could have calamitous repercussions for the Partnership.

'It's right,' Baker said. 'He set me up. He turned over all the analysts' reports to the directors *without* showing them to me. So I walked into a Board Meeting like an idiot – totally unprepared – and they just chewed me up.'

'He did this on purpose?' Leland said; he looked uncomprehendingly at his old friend. *How could they do this?* he thought. It was unthinkable. Tom Baker *was* Feldcore. His father – an iron-jawed pioneer with a pedigree that went back to the old Forty-Niners – had built up the conglomerate from a corner dime-store in old L.A., before Prohibition, when there were still mule-carts on the Hollywood Hills and a girl had to be certified a virgin by a Studio doctor before they'd allow her to work in the new movies. And today Feldcore was practically a State institution, employing thousands of people . . .

Tom Baker shook his head slowly. 'Oh, yeah – they did it on purpose all right. Then I find out last night that Wendle asked to see the Board privately, where he tells them I've lost control.' He leant forward across the desk, looking at McKenzie with desperate urgency. 'They've called a final meeting for next week, Leland, and it doesn't look good.'

McKenzie nodded judiciously, sat thinking for a moment, then said, 'Let me make a few phone calls, Tom – see what I can find out.'

Tom Baker paused, sweating again. He looked oddly helpless – which was so far from his usual style that it was almost pathetic. Used to unchallenged power and authority, he'd been taken so unawares by this sudden *putsch* that the shock had knocked him completely off-balance. McKenzie realised he was looking at a near-broken man. He was going to have to work fast, and if necessary pull a few clever tricks, if he was going to save the man's corporate skin.

Baker was suddenly embarrassed. 'I don't mean to drag you in, Leland . . . This is really an in-house battle. It's just that' – he paused, wiping his face again with the big handkerchief – 'well, I'll tell you this . . . if Steven Wendle becomes Chief Executive in my place, he's gonna give the legal work to another firm.'

McKenzie nodded grimly. He'd already guessed as much – Tom Baker was a proud man and wouldn't have come round to ask for Leland's help if there hadn't been a tie-up with the firm. Nevertheless, hearing the man say the words sent a chill to McKenzie's heart. He pursed his lips. 'Like I said – let me make a few phone calls.'

*

Leland McKenzie's bedroom was large, comfortably furnished and slightly impersonal, as was to be expected of an elderly bachelor of austere and settled habits. What light touches there were – a Chinese vase full of dried flowers, an Andrew Wyeth reproduction, elegant hairbrushes and make-up pencils and face creams spread carelessly across the dressing table – had been supplied by Rosalind Shays.

Shorn of her padded shoulders and severe business suit – her make-up replaced by glistening night cream, and her hair hanging freely over a rather fetching pink silk nightdress – she looked less intimidating, almost demure, as she lay in the big double bed, waiting for Leland to join her. He came out of the bathroom en suite, wearing his dark blue pyjamas buttoned up to the neck like a school uniform, and stood for a moment by the bed, conscientiously sawing between his teeth with dental floss.

A stranger, breaking into the bedroom unawares, might have put them down as a securely married couple of many years' standing. Although their relationship was comparatively recent, and had been undertaken with a certain stealth and secrecy (in an effort to escape the inevitable censure of Leland's colleagues in the office), it was not without passion, even love.

Rosalind Shays was a typically modern American woman whose driving ambition and success had long outstripped her capacity to enjoy any serenity in her mature years. In short, she'd begun to panic at the awful possibility of facing a lonely, loveless old age. Leland McKenzie seemed to fit the bill perfectly. He was not a bad-looking man; he was neat and tidy, and highly personable; he was intelligent, successful, gainfully employed and well-off, if not exactly rich, by Californian standards; and he enjoyed great authority and respect in the community.

None of Rosalind's associates and contacts – she was a woman who had associates rather than friends – was likely to disapprove of him. He was thoughtful, serious and *kind*. For Rosalind Shays was not a woman who'd ever attracted much kindness – probably because she'd never seemed to need it. Efficiency, success, results – those had been *the bottom line* to her existence – the gamut of her life, from A to B . . .

She was happy with Leland, and he was blissfully happy with her. What was more, they'd discovered, quite early on and to their shared surprise, that they were well suited in

73

bed. For Rosalind this had been a blessed relief. Leland might be no Valentino; but he was considerate, patient, even quite passionate.

Leland was happy too. More than happy, he was ecstatic, and for weeks now, he'd been feeling ten – even twenty – years younger. But tonight his equanimity was shadowed by the memory of his encounter that day with Tom Baker, of Feldcore Consolidated. McKenzie tried not to bring his office troubles home – at least, not to bed – but this was different. The problem was not only pressing, it was imperative. If Baker lost out, then the Partnership lost out too – and that was not only serious, it was potentially catastrophic. If McKenzie Brackman lost the Feldcore account, it could mean a shortfall of up to twenty percent on the firm's annual turnover, and that in turn could gravely undermine their credit-worthiness with the bank.

But McKenzie knew that if he was to save Baker, and keep the Feldcore account, he was going to need help. More than that, he was going to need genius. And that meant more than the bright, squeaky-clean integrity of the team he'd built up at McKenzie Brackman. For Leland was uncomfortably aware – as he screwed up the waxy thread of dentifloss and threw it in the wastepaper basket by the bed – that in order to win out against these sharks at Feldcore, he might have to be prepared to use unorthodox tactics.

The idea didn't please him: but the idea of the firm going down the chute pleased him far less. He said, as he climbed in next to Rosalind, 'Honey, I've got a problem.'

'I know,' she said.

'Oh? Does it show that bad?'

'It shows. Tell me about it.'

He told her, repeating exactly what Tom Baker had said

in the office, and emphasising what the loss of Feldcore was likely to mean for the firm. 'According to Don Orey, Wendle has four of the seven Board votes locked up,' he said finally.

'I can't believe that,' she said calmly. 'Tom Baker *is* Feldcore.'

'Not any more. Wendle's smear campaign has poisoned him pretty good.'

She turned towards him, resting her head on her arm. 'So go after Wendle. Anybody that dirty has to have left some tracks.'

'I don't know,' he said, frowning.

'Let me see the files, Leland. There has to be something to impeach him with.'

'I don't want to stoop to that level,' he said, more for the record than with any conviction.

Rosalind smiled at him grimly. 'Leland, Feldcore is your biggest client. You've just said it yourself – if Feldcore goes, you *lose* that client. You'll be forced to make lay-offs, maybe. You damn well better fight here . . .'

'Yeah,' he said wearily. He was badly worried. He was going to have to fight dirty; and to this end, the means were readily to hand – a few inches away, lying in his own bed. For Rosalind Shays, besides being his lover, was a shrewd and ruthless operator.

Her method of work wasn't exactly his style: but then drastic problems called for drastic solutions. Leland decided that he had no choice in the matter. He kissed her and turned out the light.

'We'll fight this together,' she said. ' 'Night, honey.'

'Good night, Rosalind.'

But Leland McKenzie did not sleep well that night.

Chapter Nine

Tommy Mullaney sat stroking his long sandy jaw, as he eyed Mrs Corrinne Becker across the Conference table. 'Ma'am,' he said at last, in his easy drawl, 'your complaint states that my client's behaviour has left you emotionally devastated. Would that be correct?'

'Yes.'

'Whose opinion is that?' Mullaney asked, almost casually.

'I guess it would be my opinion.' Corrinne's eyes smouldered as she spoke: yet at the same time she cringed in her chair. The object of her wrath and contempt sat a few feet away, next to Tommy Mullaney.

Arnie Becker sat quiet, sober, desolate; he hated what was happening, but felt he must put on the bravest face possible. As Tommy had said to him, before the meeting, 'You make your bed, Arnie – you gotta sleep in it . . .'

Mullaney now looked at Becker's wife and said, as kindly as he could, 'You weren't caused to seek therapy or any psychiatric counselling for this emotional devastation?'

Corrinne's hands, clasped tightly together, writhed slightly on the table in front of her. 'No, I wasn't.'

Beside her, sat her attorney: a dark, solid man in an expensive striped suit with padded shoulders – a gangster's suit. He was called Kyle Santars, and he had a reputation for being good at his job – at the rough end of the divorce business.

He had several big gold rings on his fingers which he tapped relentlessly against the table top while Mullaney questioned Corrinne. Tommy surmised that the man had been retained by Corrinne's parents, as a kind of revenge against poor Arnie, of whom they'd never much approved. Santars sat watching Mullaney with a morose black stare, as the interview with Corrinne continued:

'So there would be no medical documentation whatsoever of your mental state at this time?' Mullaney asked her.

'No, there wouldn't.'

'Very good.' Tommy tried not to look at Becker while he spoke; he hated doing this – almost as much as his client did – but he still couldn't help feeling that Arnie had been asking for it . . . The man was a damn fool. But Mullaney also had a job to do – to look after Arnie Becker's best interests. With his quiet, sleepy eyes still on the injured wife, he pressed on, 'Now you were married to your *first* husband for how long, Mrs Becker?'

'Seven years.'

'Did the separation from this man cause you any emotional distress?'

Corrinne glanced nervously at Santars, who just shrugged his huge padded shoulders, still staring darkly at Mullaney. 'Um' – she hesitated – 'yes . . . I'm sure it did.'

'But you recovered fully,' Mullaney said.

'I don't know' – her fingers writhed as though in pain, her eyes darting about the room – 'I guess I . . .'

'Well then' – Mullaney's eyes crinkled into a friendly smile – 'might some of the emotional damage you suffer today be the product of *that* event?'

'No. I recovered from that event.' Her reply was controlled – too controlled.

'Okay. So we're talking about a kind of pain you do, in fact, recover from.'

'The trauma was much worse this time!' Corrinne cried defensively. 'He . . .'

'How is the break-up of a nine-month marriage more traumatic than that of a seven-*year* marriage?'

Corrinne's lips trembled, 'Because having been once divorced, I was much more emotionally unstable this time.'

'You have full custody of your daughter, Chloe, d'you not – Ms Hammond?'

'Yes' – it was almost a whisper.

'Subject to modification at any time,' Mullaney added, 'do you consider yourself to be an unstable person, Ms Hammond?'

Corrinne's hand flew up to her mouth. 'Oh, God!' – her eyes were wide with terror – 'Is this what you're gonna try? – you think you can take my daughter away?'

'We're just concerned with your emotional fitness,' Mullaney said drily.

'There's nothing wrong with my emotional fitness, Mr Mullaney – I just . . .'

'You just want to get even with my client,' Tommy said, nodding.

Kyle Santars tried to break in here, growling, 'All right – let's . . .'

Mullaney cut him off, 'C'mon, Ms Hammond – that's what this is all about, isn't it? You don't have that much mental anguish – you haven't sought *any* psychiatric treatment. And given the settlement we've offered, this couldn't be about money. So why are we here?'

'*Why are we here?*' she repeated; she was close to hysteria now. 'He sleeps with a childhood friend of mine the week of our wedding. Then with a client while I'm throwing a party for him on his birthday. And you ask, *Why are we here . . .?*'

Kyle Santars made a lugubrious gesture, as though to restrain her; and Mullaney said, 'So you want him to hurt, Ms Hammond?'

'Yeah, I want him to hurt!' Corrinne screamed.

'Corrinne – please,' Santars said, frowning. The last thing he wanted was an hysterical harridan on his hands; but she wasn't taking anyone's advice. She was half out of her chair now, yelling at Mullaney like a woman demented:

'And maybe if he hurts enough, he won't be able to even *think* of this marriage without wanting to cry! 'Cause that's that it's like for me, Mr Mullaney – and that's why the hell we're here!'

Throughout this outburst Arnie Becker sat forward, his chin resting on his hands, his blue eyes gazing at the far wall of the Conference room. Towards the end, he'd almost stopped listening; and the suntanned skin on either side of his slightly receding hairline had begun to sweat.

*

It was quiet in the restaurant, at the top end of Rodeo Drive – still too early for the lunchtime crowd.

Rosalind Shays sat at a corner table, away from the bar,

79

tucking into a plate of *pâté de campagne* with quails' eggs. She was dressed in a black cutaway dress that managed to be both sexy and business-like at the same time.

Seated opposite her was a middle-aged man with a heavy, handsome face and soft ash-grey hair that showed up silver under the restaurant lighting. His name was Steven Wendle, and he was one of the new Vice-Presidents of Feldcore Consolidated.

He was eating with neat, precise movements, chewing each mouthful a given number of times. Rosalind guessed he'd been reared as a tough kid on the wrong side of the tracks, and his table manners – like his immaculate clothes – were from the most exclusive mail-order catalogue on the market.

He laid his fork down and said, 'Remember – I still don't know you. Why should I bother to trust you?'

She smiled, 'Maybe you just have to take a chance, Mr Wendle. Anyone ambitious enough to go after Feldcore certainly must be willing to take chances.'

'Uh-huh,' Wendle dabbed a napkin fastidiously to his full lips. 'And what exactly is in this for you?' he added, in a rich low baritone, smooth with elocution lessons.

'Leland McKenzie is a close personal friend of mine. Losing Feldcore would seriously threaten his firm – maybe even his own job.'

Wendle cocked a thick silver eyebrow. 'So?' He looked about as sympathetic as a black mamba contemplating its lunch.

'I help you overthrow Tom Baker – you promise to leave Feldcore's business at McKenzie Brackman after you become Chief Executive Officer.'

Wendle sat for a moment watching her with dark

glittering eyes. At last, he leaned forward and said carefully, 'First of all, Ms Shays, I'm not sure I need your help. Second . . .'

'You have a one-vote lead with the Board,' she said, dropping all sweetness from her voice. 'Right now, it's tenuous at best. I have information which – in your hands – would make Baker resign without a fight.'

'I'm listening,' Wendle said softly.

'Through my relationship with Leland McKenzie, I got access to files this morning – business and personal. I found evidence of a certain vice crime, committed by Mr Baker, as well as evidence of a possible cover-up.'

Wendle moistened his full lips. 'What kind of cover-up?' He sounded interested now.

Rosalind pretended to hesitate. 'I'm not sure. A memo makes clear he was arrested for three counts of solicitation – one with a minor. But there's no public record of it at the D.A.'s office. But there's also a *second* memo which talks about a pay-off to a district attorney – identified only by initials. My thinking is, there had to be a bribe.' She leaned forward herself, until they were close enough to kiss.

'Now – I'll give you these memos, Mr Wendle – but you'll have to pretend you got them elsewhere.' She paused while a waiter cleared away the first course, and a second waiter served the *tournedos rossini* with thin, corrugated, crisp potatoes and fresh artichoke hearts flown in from France the night before. (At least, that's what the menu said.)

Wendle's handsome, fleshy face could hardly contain his excitement. 'You think this will make Tom Baker roll?'

Rosalind sat forward and sliced the steak knife into her tournedo, like a dagger. 'Call a meeting,' she said. 'I'll get myself invited to it by Leland – ostensibly to lend him support. You drop the bomb – then I, in my infinite wisdom, will objectively advise that he can't risk letting this become public.' She put a fat slice of steak into her mouth and winked roguishly at him. 'You'll be Chief Executive, Mr Wendle, by the end of the week. In return, you guarantee Feldcore's business to McKenzie Brackman.'

Wendle touched his napkin again to his mouth. 'It can't be as simple as that,' he murmured, only half convinced.

'Oh, yes it can!' Rosalind cried – knowing that nine times out of ten the quasi-criminal mind is a greedy mind, and that greed leads to recklessness. 'And if, for some reason, they turn *down* your business, you guarantee it to *my* firm – minimum of two years.'

She'd played it beautifully – although Wendle was just a shade too dumb to see just *how* beautifully. He might not have trusted her if she'd appeared to be hooking just for McKenzie's sake: but naked self-interest was something he understood absolutely.

He nodded and sat back grinning. '*Wow!* You're every bit as good as they say!'

She frowned. 'I beg your pardon?'

He began to chuckle, 'You know damn well if I unseat Baker with these kinds of tactics, Leland McKenzie wouldn't *touch* my business – he'd rather die than get into bed with me! This isn't about helping *him* – it's about helping *you!* Very deft.' He went on nodding and grinning. 'Very deft indeed, Ms Shays.'

Rosalind took another mouthful of the tender red tournedo. 'There's an offer on the table, Mr Wendle. Either accept it or reject it.'

He sighed. 'Okay. You got a deal, Ms Shays.'

She gave him a brilliant smile. 'Please – call me Ros!'
He smiled back. 'You got a deal, Ros.'

Chapter Ten

The blinds were drawn against the yellow light filtering through the gritty smog outside; and the air-conditioning hummed gently, like the engines of a great ship. Suddenly Becker spoke:

'Could I —' He was sweating slightly, although the room was cool. 'Could I talk to Corrinne – alone – for a minute?'

Kyle Santars frowned. 'I don't think that's wise.'

Becker looked imploringly at his wife. 'Corrinne – please? Sooner or later, you and I *have* to talk.'

She stared bleakly at the table. 'Okay,' she said, in a small voice.

Becker turned to the two attorneys. 'Would you both excuse us?'

Tommy Mullaney shrugged, 'Okay,' he said. *What the hell*, he thought: he didn't care much, one way or the other. If Corrinne Hammond Becker wanted to tear the emotional guts out of her husband – or they now wanted to kiss and make up – what difference did it make to him? He was just a well-paid toreador handling the cape, with poor Arnie as the bull.

Becker waited till both attorneys were out of the room,

then turned to his wife, his eyes pleading like a dog that knows it's about to be taken away and put down.

'I miss you,' he said.

Her lips quivered. 'I miss you too, Arnie.'

'Look, I . . .'' – the words clogged in his throat – 'I think I've been in the divorce business long enough to know what's going on here. And —'

'Are you going to tell me what I'm feeling now, Arnie?'

'No,' he said. He hesitated. 'I guess I'm wondering . . . since I've *admitted* that I screwed up, since I've pleaded with you to take me back . . . I'm just wondering why you want to be so punishing.'

'Tell me about punishing,' she said; and there was a flicker of anger in her voice.

Becker winced. 'Corrinne, I don't want a fight here. Drop the guard for one second and just *talk* to me. Please – if we're gonna be leaving each other's lives, talk to me once before you go.'

Corrinne stared at him but said nothing. He couldn't decide whether she just didn't know what to say, or knew but didn't trust herself in the act of saying it. When she did at last speak, her voice was tired, empty of all emotion, 'Do you know how much you hurt me?' she said.

He looked at her forlornly. 'Yes,' he said softly. He took a step forward, reached out for her. 'We can give it another chance, Corrinne.'

'I've tried to convince myself of that Arnie. But I can't.'

'Please' – he tried to reach her, hold her, but she flinched away – 'Why can't we just try again?'

'Because . . .' Her voice had hardened again. 'Because as much as I love you, Arnie, I don't respect you. I don't trust you. And that's never going to change.'

'Can't we just separate for a while? I mean . . . why . . .?'

'No. No, Arnie. I have to be done. I can't live in the middle of this, any more. I can't survive where I am now. Let's just get it over with.'

'What'd you tell Chloe?' he gulped.

'That you won't be living with us any more. She'd like to see you, though. To say goodbye.'

Becker felt as though the ground had given way under his feet. 'We're really over – aren't we?' he said weakly.

'Yeah,' she said. 'We're over, Arnie.' And she swallowed back the tears; but her eyes were still dry.

*

Leland McKenzie was distinctly nervous. And not just about the way the meeting would go – whether he'd succeed in having Tom Baker's hide, and so keep the Feldcore account for the firm.

No. What really worried him – worried them all – was that none of them had done this kind of thing before. They say all lawyers have to be actors, up to a point; but this was different – on an altogether grander scale. This was going to be a full-scale *production*.

They'd all rehearsed their parts, over and over, until they were word-perfect. All, that is, except Wendle and his lawyer. They were to be the loose cannons here; and as any experienced director could have told Leland, even the most free-style Method Acting cannot guard against a rogue one-liner that can wreck the whole show.

Another thing worried Leland, but only slightly, and much less than he'd have expected it to have done, up to a few days ago. The ethics of the thing – whether, in his desperation to rescue McKenzie Brackman's account with Feldcore, he wasn't compromising his own high standards of integrity and straight dealing.

Perhaps it was the influence of Rosalind? He hoped not. Or fear of creeping financial ruin? Perhaps . . . yes, that was it. Maybe he was just getting hardened, cynical, like the worse of them. All for the quick buck, the Mighty Dollar, he thought; and shuddered.

*

They were all together in McKenzie's room: Rosalind, Ann Kelsey, Tom Baker, Steven Wendle, and Wendle's own personal attorney – a stout, soft-faced young man called Kevin Wilkes, whom McKenzie hadn't met before but whose type he recognised too well: an ambitious young lawyer who would be honest up to the point where it paid him and his client to be slightly less than honest. In other words, a fairly regular, average L.A. lawyer. Not like Leland McKenzie – oh, not at all . . .

McKenzie had taken his place at the head of the table. The curtain was up.

'All right, ladies, gentlemen. If you'd all be seated, please.' He found the polite formality of the introduction quite natural: a sporting chivalry between rivals about to be pitted in deadly combat.

His friend, Tom Baker, smiled at Wendle, 'Steven! How nice . . .'

'Tom! Well, well – good little team assembled . . .'

'You've been organising a few troops, yourself,' Baker said, with grim cheerfulness.

Wendle chucked; as Ann Kelsey broke in, brisk and

87

business-like, 'All right – let's not waste everybody's time.' She looked at Steven Wendle, 'You said you had a proposal?'

'Yes,' Wendle settled into his chair and smiled at Tom Baker. 'And it's very simple. We avoid a nasty and divisive fight in front of the Board next week, by you voluntarily stepping down today.'

'And why would I do that?' Baker said, the lines round his eyes and mouth tightening.

In contrast, Wendle's fleshy features became fuller, almost voluptuous. 'To avoid a public and private humiliation, Baker.'

Tom Baker stared at him, all chivalry between them gone now. '*What?*' he cried.

'That's right,' Wendle said. 'Humiliation caused by the revelation three years ago of your arrest for soliciting prostitutes.'

This time Baker jumped as though he'd found a snake on his chair. '*What!*' he yelled again, as Ann Kelsey let out her breath in a low gasp.

Wendle was chuckling again, thoroughly enjoying himself now. 'We have evidence of your bribing a district attorney to get the charges dismissed – money which most likely came out of Feldcore funds.'

'I don't know what the hell you're talking about!' Baker blurted, slumping back in his chair.

Wendle waved a hand dismissively. 'Forget it, Tom – it's over. I have connections with certain people at the D.A.'s office.' He brought a couple of documents out of his hip pocket and shook them across the table, under Baker's face:

'Here's a copy of the secret memo your lawyers sent to a certain Assistant District Attorney "L.T.". Initials only' –

and he winked conspiratorially round the table – 'laying out all the details in black and white.'

'Let me see that!' Rosalind snapped, leaning across the table.

'This is blackmail,' Baker said, 'I'm not letting . . .'

Wendle cut him short, 'This is me thinking of the good of the company, Tom,' he cried triumphantly. 'Something this serious *has* to be brought to the Board's attention' – he paused, eyeing the haggard Baker, and the apparently, equally shocked Ann Kelsey beside him –' . . . *unless* – and he gave them both a sly, mock-friendly smile – 'unless, of course, you agree to step down . . .'

'You won't get away with this!' Baker roared; and there was a wild, dangerous glare in his eyes.

Rosalind cut in, with a voice like dry ice, 'Assuming you *can* prove this . . . what sort of deal would you be prepared to make, Mr Wendle?'

Tom Baker banged the table, before Wendle had time to answer, 'I'm not making *any deal*!'

'You may have to, Tom,' Rosalind said. She stared at Baker with a look of grim resignation. 'My God . . . if this is true,' she muttered. Baker seemed stunned.

So did Leland McKenzie. He looked sadly across at his lover and shook his head. 'Very good, Rosalind. Very good indeed.' She looked inquiringly at him, as he went on, 'When you asked me to look at the file the other night, I didn't quite trust you. God knows – I *wanted* to, Rosalind. But I didn't.'

'What are you talking about?' she asked him crossly; but there was also an uneasiness in her voice.

McKenzie looked at her, weary but determined. 'I'm talking about the fact that Tom Baker was *never* arrested

89

for solicitation. I wrote those memos myself the other day and planted them in the file. I wanted to see what you'd do with them.'

Ann Kelsey was the first to speak. She turned, her voice stiff with puritanical venom: 'You lying, conniving bitch!' she yelled at Rosalind Shays.

McKenzie, as though too wounded by betrayal, did not even protest. He just went on looking sorrowfully at Rosalind, while Wendle gaped helplessly at his young attorney, then back to the table.

'Will someone please explain what's . . .' he began.

'Stop talking, Mr Wendle,' McKenzie said; he was still looking at Rosalind, who flinched as though trying to avoid his eyes. 'Was it to see me fall?' he went on. 'Was it all a charade just to . . .?' He sounded almost grief-stricken as he spoke; his eyes seemed to be saying that the betrayal's bad enough; but the humiliation is unbearable . . .

He turned now to his friend, Baker, 'Look, Tom, they've got nothing on you.' And to the rest of the table: 'There's no reason to entertain this meeting any longer.' He stood up. 'If you'll excuse me . . .'

Rosalind, appearing shaken but still determined to retrieve the situation, said quickly, 'Leland – just a moment. It was to *help* you . . .'

But McKenzie was already walking to the door. Pale, drooping, shattered: it was a magnificent performance.

She called after him, again, 'Hey, Leland, wait! The deal was, he was going to keep Feldcore's business here. It was all done for *you*!'

McKenzie gave a weary shrug. 'Even if that's true' – he paused, his hand on the door handle, as he nodded at Tom Baker – 'you tried to destroy him in the process.'

Rosalind seemed temporarily nonplussed, 'I'm sorry,' she said.

Wendle, meanwhile, had sagged visibly in his chair; he looked again at his attorney, Wilkes, but said nothing. As a man who was used to fighting dirty, Steven Wendle knew the score. He was beaten, licked, K.O.'d – by this shrewd, clever, straight-arrow McKenzie who'd got him in a tiger's claw and there was nothing he could do about it. Useless to try and fight back; he couldn't even move.

Leland McKenzie walked out and closed the door behind him. In the silence, Wilkes turned at last to his client, 'You got that memo from her?' he asked, in a low voice.

Wendle said impatiently, 'C'mon, let's go' – and stood up.

'Hold on a second!' said Ann Kelsey. 'The deal's just changed.' She fixed Steve Wendle with a fierce glare: '*You're* the one who's resigning from the company, Wendle. And if you don't, *we're* going public with your little blackmailing scheme, and you'll be thrown out without any settlement at all.'

'Hey!' – Wendle had gone very white – 'You guys made up the lies here, not me! I . . .'

'But you tried to use them for extortion,' Ann Kelsey said. 'You promised Feldcore's business to us, in exchange for this information. You think your Board of Directors will stand for that?' She looked at Wendle with a look of withering contempt. 'You make me sick.' Then she turned to Rosalind, 'As for *you*' – she gave a disdainful shrug – 'I admire your consistency.'

Wilkes began to speak, hurriedly, to his boss, 'Let me put together some severance numbers. Then . . .'

'Hey, Kevin, I'm not takin' this —' Wendle began.

'*Be quiet*, Steven! Just keep your mouth shut,' Wilkes said. He stood up and turned to Ann Kelsey: he knew his client was in bad trouble, and as his attorney he was going to have to work fast. 'I'll get back to you with a proposal,' he said to her; then, without another word, he led Steven Wendle quickly out of the room.

Ann got up and closed the door abruptly behind them both. Then she turned and looked at Rosalind, who began to beam triumphantly at her. They'd all been splendid – every one of them word-perfect, right on cue. Hollywood would have been proud of them!

Ann began to smile too, just as the communicating door into Douglas Brackman's office opened. Leland McKenzie stood there, peering expectantly at them all, slightly nervous. 'Well?' he asked.

'It worked,' Ann said, with a delighted, exhausted sigh.

'Yes?' McKenzie's eyebrows rose; but he still sounded uneasy.

Tom Baker sat there, mopping his face with his big handkerchief, and began slowly shaking his head, 'I must say, you guys are something!'

Ann put her hands on the table. 'Rosalind – you were incredible. Brilliant!'

'*Me?*' – Rosalind Shays gave a small shrug – 'What about Leland here? Did you see *his* performance? Worthy of an Oscar!'

McKenzie came into the room, pausing in front of his friend, Tom Baker, 'Congratulations, Tom.' But he sounded a lot less elated than the others.

Baker sprang up and suddenly folded his old friend in a massive bear-hug. 'Thank you, Leland! Thank you!'

They all broke into joyous, uninhibited laughter – all

except McKenzie. He still looked uneasy, even unhappy. This wasn't the way he'd learnt to do things at Law School: why, he'd spent a lifetime trying to build up a solid, decent, God-fearing practice. It was against all his instincts, all his better judgement . . . it was *dirty*.

He said, 'All right, guys. Fun's over. Let's get back to work.' He didn't look at Rosalind as he spoke.

Chapter Eleven

The stairs and hallway were almost in darkness. Arnie Becker crept up the stairs with the stealth of a burglar. He was very nervous: his stomach muscles were knotted, his legs felt they could hardly take his weight, and he knew he was sweating again. He was sweating a lot these days; and he worried not only about his mental state but the possibility that he was cracking up physically as well.

Corrinne was following him up the stairs. A few steps below the landing, he turned and asked, in a hoarse whisper, 'She knows I'm coming?'

Corrinne nodded, 'Yeah.'

Becker paused at the door at the top of the stairs. He hesitated, braced himself, then stepped forward and, without knocking, walked softly into his stepdaughter's room, 'Hey. . .!' he smiled bravely.

The little girl was sitting up in bed; she was carefully combing the long flaxen hair of a big blue-eyed doll. She was in her nightdress but her legs were drawn up under her chin, outside the covers. 'Hi, Arnie,' she said, with that slightly off-hand innocence of the very young.

'Hi, sweetheart,' Arnie said, sitting down on the edge of

the bed; he hoped the pink light from the bedside lamp wasn't shining too obviously on his damp brow. 'I've missed you,' he added. Then smiled again, coaxingly, 'C'mon – let's get you properly into bed, under the covers. It's *my* job to tuck you in tonight – and I'm gonna do it right.'

He watched her start to climb under the covers. 'Why do you have to leave, Arnie?' she asked.

'Well, honey, it's kinda complicated. It's uh . . . well, your mom and I feel it's best for me not to live here. And . . .' – he found the words catching in his throat.

'Is Mommy making you leave?' she said.

'No. No – uh . . .' – he patted the bedclothes round her and sat down again, drawing closer – 'Listen, honey – you gotta understand it's my fault that this happening. Now your mother – she's gonna need you to be extra good for a while 'cause this is a little hard for everybody. You and I are gonna make a secret pact, where you help take care of her – okay?'

''Kay,' she said, snuggling down under the covers.

Arnie reached down to adjust the blanket round her little shoulders; as he did so, he noticed that his hand was trembling. His arm felt like a lump of lead. *Oh God*, he thought. This was worse than the heaviest case, with the lousiest brief, before the most hostile judge. He'd rather face a charge of contempt than have to plead this one . . .

'Now you're okay,' he went on, very gently, struggling to keep his voice on track. 'Don't you go kicking this blanket off tonight, will you? It's gonna be cold – and we don't want you getting pneumonia.' He patted Chloe's head, then smoothed his unsteady hand over the doll's nylon hair. 'We don't want Tracey here coming down with anything either, do we?'

'Are you ever coming back?' she said.

'Not to live, I don't think.' He paused; his nose felt blocked, his tear-ducts jamming; and he thought he was either going to sneeze or break down. He could hardly get the next words out. 'I love you very much, honey.'

'I love you too,' she said; and suddenly reached up and hugged him. For a few seconds he held her tight against him, and his whole body felt as weak as water.

Outside the door, he knew Corrinne was waiting, silently in the dark, and he could hear her crying. Suddenly he could bear it no longer. He let go of the child, stood up and stumbled to the door; then, like a man fleeing the scene of some terrible crime, he began to rush down the stairs, across the passage, reaching the front door before the tears came. He just managed to make it outside, into the chill night air, where he broke down altogether and began crying like a baby.

*

That same evening Jonathan Rollins was out for his evening run. It was a quiet residential street, just inland from Venice and the beach; and the chill air was full of the bitter-sweet scene of orange blossom and frangipani.

It was a good evening for running; the night air was cool in his lungs and the tracksuit felt loose and easy on him. Rollins was in good condition and was hardly sweating, as he started on the long stretch up to Brentwood Drive and the row of late-night *de luxe* shops that sold liquor and guns and delicatessen takeaways to L.A.'s affluent alcoholics, sportsmen and couch-potatoes.

Suddenly he had the wary sensation of being followed. The hairs on his neck prickled and he glanced over his shoulder. Nobody behind him. Yet seconds later his shadow was silhouetted by the bright lights of a car which swished along the quiet street behind him. Rollins continued his even strides. Still his shadow danced before him, stark against the harsh white sidewalk. He ran on, then felt tension building in his muscles. What was wrong? What was his body telling him?

Of course! The car should have overtaken him long ago, yet it dawdled along behind him. He risked a glance over his shoulder. This time the light had changed. It was red, and it had started flashing like an angry pulse. Instinctively – and perhaps through a cautious fear – he slowed down; and as he did so, the car behind accelerated, drew level, cruised a few yards, then suddenly cut across him and pulled up. Both doors snapped open on either side. Two men got out. They were in uniform.

They came strolling towards him. He stood quite still, trying to control his breathing, knowing exactly how to handle the situation. It happened all the time in this city. *Christ!* – if he, Jonathan Rollins, ace-attorney, couldn't handle an incident like this, he'd better pack up and get back over the tracks . . .

He looked both men in the eye. One of them flashed a light in his face and he was temporarily blinded. All he could see of them was that they were big, unsmiling, and they were both white. 'Evening, officers' – he sounded over-relaxed, almost jaunty – 'was I over the limit . . .?'

The light moved, with menacing slowness, down over his

tracksuit, on to his designer trousers. 'Let's see some I.D.,' one of them growled.

'I don't have my wallet. I don't carry it when I run.'

One of them moved forward. 'Step towards the car, please. Slowly.'

'I'm an attorney,' Rollins began, 'I live two miles from here . . .'

'Yeah, sure,' said the second one. 'Move.'

Rollins didn't exactly panic. He remained very calm, very professional. 'I'm an attorney,' he repeated. 'What's your reasonable suspicion?'

'You don't belong here,' the second one said. 'You don't fit the profile of the neighbourhood – *that's* my suspicion.' He was shorter, thicker than the first man – his heavy brutish face reflected upwards from the light, like a hairless pig's snout. *Pig!* thought Rollins wildly, remembering the old Sixties' slang and thinking how apt it was . . .

'We asked you to move towards the car,' the man said; and suddenly grabbed the front of Rollins' tracksuit.

'Hey! Get your hands off me . . .!'

'*Shut your mouth!*' the officer said, with evident relish, just as Rollins twisted and for a moment slipped free; but the policeman moved with surprising speed, grabbed him from behind and started to yank his arms up in a choke-hold.

The pain was sudden and excrutiating, and Rollins went mad. 'You bastard,' he said, not very loudly; then jerked sideways, slipped again under the man's heavy grasp, and was free just long enough to take a wild swing at the snout-like face and felt his knuckles connect with a hard satisfying click against the man's stubbly jaw.

The first man moved in fast, with a punch to Rollins'

kidneys which dropped him to his knees. His anger was temporarily dissipated by the sickening pain; he felt dazed, losing consciousness. Snout-face had stepped back, and stood clasping his injured jaw with both hands; while the first man began dragging Rollins, floppy-legged, unresisting, towards the squad-car where he was hauled upright and his face slammed down hard against the cold vinyl hood.

'Happy now, smart guy?' – he grabbed Rollins' short woolly head and yanked it upwards, grinning cruelly. '*You happy now?*' He had a lean, mean face, and Rollins thought for a moment of yelling for help, then saw the rows of quiet, darkened houses behind the smart lines of orderly trees; and he knew, with the instincts of his race, that no-one here would come out to help a poor black boy who'd just taken a swing at a copy and was now being bundled into the squad-car . . .

He was on his own now; and, as they kicked one leg away from under him and pushed him head-first into the car, he felt himself slide into merciful oblivion.

*

At the next Morning Conference, Jonathan Rollins was the only one not present. Douglas Brackman, in the chair, made a mental note of it but deferred comment. Ten minutes, on, Roxanne came in; she looked flustered.

'Douglas – sorry . . .'

'Yes?'

'Jonathan is calling in,' she said breathlessly. 'He's in jail.'

There was an audible intake of breath round the whole table. '*What!*' – '*How?*' – '*Why?*'

'He was arrested,' she said quickly. 'Said he left a message on Victor's machine last night.

Sifuentes reddened, with a quickly, guilty glance at Grace Van Owen who pretended not to notice. 'I didn't get it,' he murmured.

'*What happened?*' Mike Kuzak cried.

'He didn't say,' Roxanne said, 'just that he's being arraigned this morning and he needs Michael or Victor.'

'I'll take it,' Sifuentes said at once, covering his guilt.

'You *both* take it,' ordered Leland McKenzie.

Brackman nodded agreement. 'Get down there – both of you. See what he needs. Grace – put in a call to District Attorney, Mike Rogoff – maybe he can help.' He looked round, 'Let's adjourn – we'll cover the other items later. Okay, move!'

They all began standing up. Arnie Becker gathered up his notes. 'What the hell could Jonathan have done?' he said quietly, articulating what everyone in the room was thinking.

Both Brackman and McKenzie looked badly troubled.

*

Assistant District Attorney Bill Graphia nodded briefly at Sifuentes and Kuzak as they entered the Arraignment Court. Old Judge Shubov was presiding – gruff but fair, looking like an old owl – as the Court bailiff brought in the young black defendant.

Jonathan Rollins looked awful: the front of his tracksuit stained with vomit, his face puffed, bruised, exhausted.

Suddenly Rollins was back in the old familiar nightmare. Gone were the smart business suits, the expense-account lunches and swish law office in downtown L.A. – he was once again the poor boy from the *barrio*, the ghetto; alone, with the whole world against him. The Court felt it too. Only Victor and Mike Kuzak, at the defendant's table, were demonstratively on his side, both looking angry but resolute.

At another table, away from the defendant and his Counsel, sat A.D.A. Zoey Clemmons – the former Mrs Tommy Mullaney – looking absurdly pretty against the austere surroundings. She was here representing the D.A.'s office; and listened aghast as the Clerk of the Court began reading the next indictment:

'Number 93571 – People versus Jonathan Rollins. Disorderly conduct – resisting arrest – aggravated assault on a police officer – two counts . . .'

Victor Sifuentes was on his feet. 'Waive reading. Defendant pleads not guilty.'

'Question of bail?' Judge Shubov asked.

'The accused,' Sifuentes said firmly, 'is a respected attorney – no criminal record – we'll be looking for O.R.'

It was the turn of A.D.A. Graphia to get to his feet. 'There's a police officer in the hospital with a broken jaw, Judge,' he said aggressively.

'And that same police officer,' Kuzak said, 'attacked Mr Rollins without provocation.'

'He resisted arrest,' Graphia said fiercely, trying to keep the conviction in his voice.

Judge Shubov looked sceptically down at the A.D.A. 'The officers wouldn't be pressing this to avoid brutality charges, would they, Mr Graphia?'

These words were music to the ears of Sifuentes and Kuzak: and to Jonathan Rollins, too, although he still felt too cowed and dejected to enjoy their full implication.

Graphia's face remained expressionless. 'The defendant assaulted a police officer,' he said flatly.

Sifuentes, taking full advantage of the opening made by the Judge's question, and determined to press home the counter-attack, said:

'We ask for a preliminary hearing at the earliest possible date . . .'

'Your Honour –' Graphia began.

'So we can refute these ridiculous charges and spare further damage to Mr Rollins' reputation,' Sifuentes said firmly.

Judge Shubov leaned forward and nodded emphatically at Sifuentes. 'Tomorrow morning, I'll do it myself.' He spoke now to the Court: 'Defendant released O.R.' – then turned to the A.D.A. – 'Sit down with your officers, Mr Graphia' – he looked sternly at a group of policemen sitting in the well of the Court, near Zoey Clemmons. 'If they made a mistake,' the judge went on, 'I don't want them compounding it in my Courtroom. Next case . . .'

Jonathan Rollins licked his lips; his mouth and throat felt like leather. It was as though his whole body had been put through a combine harvester. Kuzak's hand closed round his elbow. 'Okay, Jonathan. Let's go . . .'

Wearily, Rollins moved between him and Sifuentes towards the door. It had gone well – so far. But there was still a long way to go. How did that phrase go? – about the mills of justice grinding small but exceeding slow . . .?

Chapter Twelve

'Okay,' said C.J., 'settle down. Just tell me what happened.'

The woman in front of her, in the client's chair, looked nervous, miserable; desperate for encouragement, for help. 'Jim took Josh for the weekend,' she began. 'Y'know, he gets him for every other weekend.'

C.J. nodded gravely, 'Yes, I know. And . . .?'

'And he's not bringing him back,' the young woman said. '*What?*'

'His lawyer just showed up this morning. He says they're bringing a new petition for custody in the Indian Court.' The young woman's eyes brimmed full of tears. Janice Long was in her late twenties – a pale, conventionally pretty girl, with her long black hair plaited and parted in the middle, Indian-style, in vague deference to her Navajo partner, now separated from her. 'Can they do this?' she added, looking tensely at C.J.

The English woman didn't answer directly. 'Where's Joshua now?'

'Still on the Reservation, with Jim.' The girl's voice was about to break into tears.

C.J., anxious to preempt any flood of emotion, pressed

rapidly on, 'Okay – look, I'll go into Court – we'll get an order.'

'When?'

'This afternoon. Leland McKenzie can get me in with Judge Lobel – and we'll jump all over this.'

Janice looked excited, grasping at straws. 'Then they'll have to give him back – right? They can't just keep him – right?'

C.J.'s face was blank. 'I don't know.'

The girl looked suddenly furious. 'What do you mean, you don't know – you're a lawyer!'

C.J. smiled patiently, 'I know the law, Janice. But I'm going to have to be honest with you – I don't know the first thing about Indians.' For a moment the two of them sat staring at each other in silence.

*

Judge Richard Lobel was a big friendly-looking man who gave the impression that he'd be a lot happier enjoying a couple of beers with the boys – or dandling his little granddaughter on his knee – than sitting up here in the stuffy Los Angeles Family Court, ready for another long day listening to all those trials and tribulations, whines and whimpers, tears and back-biting resentments and hatreds.

Below him, in the well of the little court, sat the handsome Native American attorney, David Wauneka, his flat brown features and long, ebony hair contrasting dramatically with his pale Givenchy suit and polka-dotted yellow silk tie. He was staring at a spot somewhere just below where Judge Lobel was sitting – deliberately ignoring

Janice Long, tense and upright, at the Petitioner's table, next to C.J.

The English lawyer was on her feet, enchanting old Judge Lobel with her Home Counties' accent: 'What Mr Long did amounts to kidnapping and . . .' when the handsome Indian broke in, with a toneless growl:

'She gave the child over to him voluntarily.'

'Because she thought it was just for a visit,' C.J. snapped back. 'She never thought he'd be held on the Reservation while —'

'Only pending a Custody Hearing, that's all,' Wauneka cut in.

'We've already *had* the Custody Hearing – and it was awarded to my client,' said C.J.

'In *your* Court,' Wauneka said. 'Now we go to *ours*.'

At this point Judge Lobel leaned forward and spoke sternly to the Indian attorney, 'Counsel, I must remind you that the order of *this* Court stands.'

The Indian's flat features betrayed no emotion, no expression at all: but his voice was full of slow, arrogant defiance. 'Your Honour, the Indian Child Welfare Act is Federal Law – it gives the Navajo tribe exclusive jurisdiction over all Indian children.'

But Judge Lobel was not going to have any attorney telling him the law in his own country. 'It's not *exclusive*, Counsel. That Act exempts final divorce decrees in our Courts – and that *includes* custody decisions and —'

'Yes, but the ruling here prejudiced my client, and the Tribal Court has decided not to afford full faith and credit.'

Judge Lobel's easy-going voice became hard, almost threatening, 'Counsel, I'm ordering you right now to bring back that boy.'

'That's not going to happen.' The Indian's face might have been carved out of a hunk of mahogany.

Judge Lobel's face swelled up like an angry bullfrog: even in these sensitive, Politically Correct, times he wasn't going to take this lying down, 'I'll lock you up for contempt,' he said grimly – noticing that not once did the Indian look him directly in the eye. For a Navajo, direct eye-contact among strangers constitutes gross incivility, and the Navajo attorney had no wish to offend this White Judge in his own Court.

He stared at the floor and said flatly, '*I'm* not the one disregarding your order.'

For a moment, Judge Lobel just glared at the impassive face below him. Then he looked at Janice Long. 'Ms Long, I'd send the police in – if I could. But I'm afraid I have no enforcement powers on the Navajo Reservation.'

'What does that mean?' she asked.

'I'm saying,' the Judge went on, 'that I can't do anything. If you want your son back any time soon, it looks like you'll have to go to the Tribal Court.'

C.J. was on her feet. 'My client is white, Your Honour. And her husband, Mr Long, is an Indian. How can we expect to get an impartial hearing in a Navajo Court?'

Judge Lobel winced. He was frustrated, enraged, but ever aware that on these tribal issues (and in front of this smooth high-powered Native American attorney), he was going to have to restrain himself; to tread mightily carefully. 'I don't know, Counsel. But since the child is currently on the Reservation, you don't have many choices.' He turned back to the Indian:

'Mr Wauneka – you tell your client, if this is the way he wants to play it, he'd better hope to hell he wins! Because I'll

106

tell you this. If Ms Long here *does* get her son back, I'll consider it my duty to cut off all unsupervised visitation.' He paused, looking back at Janice Long. 'I wish I could be more help, Ma'am. But you'll have to take your case to the Navajo Court.'

C.J. looked sympathetically at her client. Janice Long was very pale, and again close to tears.

*

The communal meeting room on the Navajo Reservation at Window Rock, Arizona, was spare and bleak – a plain wooden table, deal chairs, concrete floor, and a single bench along the back wall.

C.J. Lamb felt overdressed, and looked it. She faced Janice Long across the table, trying to comfort her, relieve her of her worst fears. It was heavy-going.

'The problem is,' she told her, 'it's not just the best interests of the child we're looking at. The Court here will be considering the welfare of the whole Tribe, as well. That's the way things work out here.'

'Then how can I possibly win?' Janice cried; she was wild, distraught.

'Well, I'm told that Navajo tradition *does* favour the mother,' C.J. said.

'Not *white* mothers, they don't! Trust me.' For a moment all the bitterness and despair showed in the girl's pale face.

'Now just listen,' C.J. said patiently. 'Whatever your attitudes are in this, Janice, you *have* to show respect in there. If you alienate the Court, we'll lose before we begin. The only thing I want them to see in you is a loving mother.'

Janice Long hung her head. 'Okay,' she said; it was almost a whisper.

'Now' – C.J. adjusted her sleeves, her manner stern and business-like – 'as for the Court. Judge William Gainser – he's a sixty-three-year-old Navajo – no legal background whatsoever. He was a Medicine Man until about three years ago, when they trained him to be a Judge.' She kept any residual irony out of her voice; but her client displayed no such restraint.

Her mouth sagged open, in shocked disbelief. 'You mean to tell me,' she cried, 'whether or not I get Joshua back depends on the say-so of a retired Medicine Man?'

As she spoke, the door opened and a big American Indian padded silently in, leading a two-year-old child. It was a little boy, black-haired, but with clear, pale features. Behind them both came the Navajo attorney, David Wauneka.

Janice turned in the same moment, and ignoring the two men, reached out to her child. 'Josh!'

'Mommy!' The child broke free of his father's grasp and rushed into the mother's arms:

'Oh, honey . . .!' – Janice's eyes were closed, as she hugged the child to her breast – 'I've missed you so much!'

Her husband, James Long, stood staring at the concrete floor. 'I wanted to let you say hi,' he said stolidly.

'Oh baby!' Janice went on, still holding the child and speaking into its ear, 'How you been, Sweetie . . .?'

'Good,' the little boy murmured, looking confused.

Janice opened her eyes and looked at her husband; her face was bleak and angry. 'How can you do this to me?' she cried.

The Indian stepped forward, folding his big arms around

108

the child and handed him gently to his attorney, Wauneka. 'Can you take him to his grandparents, please,' he said to the lawyer.

Without a word or change of expression, Wauneka led the child, unprotesting, out of the room. Janice stared after him, stricken.

James looked blankly at his young wife. 'I'm sorry. I didn't want to do it this way, but —'

Janice balled her fists at her side, her voice almost a scream, 'You kidnapped him! You lied to me, and you —'

'I want to raise my son, Janice.'

'He lives with *me*!' his wife yelled.

'Not any more, he doesn't,' the Indian said.

Janice was white and shaking. 'Now you listen to me Jimmy! I don't care what Court we're in . . . I'm not going to let you win! I will fight as long and hard as I have to . . .' Her voice broke into sobs, 'You're not taking away my little boy! You're not doing this – he's all I have . . .!'

'He's all I have too,' the Indian said, the pain showing only in his eyes.

Janice gave him a weak, imploring look. 'Please. Please . . .'

Her husband's face held about as much expression as the furniture around them. 'I'm sorry.' He turned and walked out of the room.

Janice stared desperately at C.J., trying again to hold back her tears. 'Get him back, C.J.,' she said, in a small pitiful voice. 'I don't care what you do. You get my son back . . .'

*

'Officer Janson,' Graphia began, in his smooth Prosecutor's voice. 'Why did you detain Mr Rollins on February 10th?'

'We had a serial rapist working the area,' the policeman replied, without expression. 'An hour earlier he beat a sixty-year-old woman half to death. The defendant matched his description.'

The Press benches of the Criminal Court were packed for the Preliminary Hearing. At the defendant's table, between Kuzak and Sifuentes, sat Jonathan Rollins, in a smart business suit, looking uncomfortable in front of him.

'What happened when you stopped Mr Rollins?' Graphia went on.

'After identifying ourselves as police officers, we asked him for identification. The suspect refused, and then became abusive and belligerent.'

'Verbally or physically?' Graphia asked.

'He called my partner a bastard, then attempted to flee the scene. When Sergeant Cobb moved to detail him, the suspect assaulted him in the face. At which point, I then subdued the suspect and placed him under arrest.'

Above them, in the gallery, a policeman in uniform, with a face like a pig's snout and his jaw wired up, sat watching keenly.

'Thank you, Officer,' Graphia said, and sat down.

Victor Sifuentes now rose. 'You thought my client was the rapist?' he said, almost casually.

Officer Jansen shrugged. 'He matched the general description.'

Sifuentes stepped forward and handed the policeman a piece of paper. 'I show you a print-out copy of the A.P.B.

report, giving a general description of the suspect. Could you read it, please.'

Jansen fingered the paper, frowning, then said, his lips hardly moving, '*Black male – height six-three – weight two hundred and twenty-five.*'

Sifuentes looked him straight in the eye. 'Mr Rollins is five-eleven and he weighs a hundred and seventy. He's four inches shorter and fifty pounds lighter, than your rapist.'

'It was dark,' Jansen said.

'And he was black,' Sifuentes countered. 'In an all-white neighbourhood.'

'Objection!' cried Graphia.

'Withdrawn,' Sifuentes said. He was still looking at the officer on the stand. 'Did you direct racial slurs to my client?'

'Nobody made any racial slurs,' Jansen said stiffly.

'Did you tell him he didn't fit the profile of the neighbourhood?'

'He didn't. This neighbourhood was white. Your client is black. We've questioned white people in black neighbourhoods, too,' he added defensively.

'Do you put them in choke-holds and punch them in the kidneys?' Sifuentes said.

'I didn't punch him,' Jansen said, with a trace of anger. '*Objection!*'

'When he broke my partner's jaw,' Jansen went on, 'I tried to restrain him and he fell against the car.'

'That's your testimony, huh? That "Mr Rollins fell against the car"?' Sifuentes said, sneering.

Jansen gave a loose shrug. 'That's what happened. Were you there?'

Sifuentes glared at him with visible disgust; then turned to Judge Shubov. 'I'm done, Your Honour.'

The judge nodded at Jansen. 'You may step down.'

The police officer left the stand and walked past the defendant's table, without a glance at either Sifuentes or Rollins.

'Anything further, Mr Graphia?' asked Judge Shubov.

'No, Your Honour.'

'Defence has asked for an immediate ruling, so I'm going to give it.' The Judge looked down at Sifuentes, 'Unfortunately, it's not the one you want. Given Officer Jansen's testimony, the signed statement of Sergeant Cobb, and their exemplary records as police officers, I find sufficient evidence to bind Mr Rollins over for trial. I'll hear Scheduling Motions tomorrow. We're adjourned.'

Sifuentes scowled with disappointment; while Jonathan Rollins just looked stunned.

Chapter Thirteen

The Navajo Tribal Court was formal and well-furnished –
nothing elaborate or fancy, but not primitive either. The
only feature that distinguished it from an ordinary City
Court was the packed rows of impassive Indian faces lining
the benches, and the Navajo flag furled beside the Stars and
Stripes. In front sat Judge William Gainser – an elderly,
soberly dressed, distinguished-looking Indian who was
listening intently to the proceedings.

James Long was on the stand, giving his testimony with
his black eyes fixed firmly on the floor in front of him.
'We'd only been back on the Reservation for eight months,
when she left. She filed for the divorce in L.A.'

Below him, at the respondent's table, Janice Long sat
stiff and immobile, next to C.J. Lamb.

David Wauneka, conspicuous and resplendent in his
European designer clothes, repeated, 'She filed for divorce
in L.A. – where she was afforded full custody and you got
visitation rights?'

'Yes,' replied Long.

'But this last time you took the child for a visit – you
decided to keep him?'

'Joshua belongs on the Reservation,' James Long said flatly.

'Why?'

'My son is a Navajo, Mr Wauneka. In the white world, he'll be raised to be ashamed of that.'

'You don't think he could be raised to appreciate his culture in Los Angeles?'

James Long retained the same expression of inscrutable blankness; only his body language hinted at contemptuous irony. 'I've lived in L.A. I've lived in many places off the Reservation. And I can tell you this – in the big cities we're thought of as uneducated, primitive . . . I don't want my son to face the hatred.'

Judge Gainser interrupted, in a low gentle voice, 'Do you think all white men hate the Indian?'

James Long turned to him, meeting his eye. 'There are two kinds. The ones who dismiss us because our skin is red. And the others, who welcome us and encourage us to be white . . .' He paused. 'I don't know which is worse.'

Wauneka nodded sympathetically. 'Do you have any reason to believe that your ex-wife would be guilty of this kind of discrimination?'

'Janice rejected the Indian world. She will raise Joshua to be white.' The Indian mask concealed the man's bitterness and sorrow. 'She will make him forget his Navajo culture.'

C.J. broke in: 'Objection. This man doesn't know my client's intent.'

'I know her,' James Long said. 'I know that she'll raise him with White Man's dreams – chasing White Man's success – and the boy will *end up* . . .' he paused, as though the words choked in his throat – 'he'll end up with White Man's contempt for the Indian.'

There was a bleak silence in the little Courtroom. 'I have nothing further,' Wauneka said, and returned to his chair.

C.J. Lamb rose. 'You, *yourself*, Mr Long, were brought up on an Indian Reservation. Yet ten years ago, you left it to pursue "White Man's success" – did you not, Mr Long?'

'I made a mistake,' the Indian said softly.

'Yes. But the truth is – growing up on a Reservation doesn't prevent one from chasing Western dreams. Does it, Mr Long?' There was a faint, determined smile on C.J.s lips as she said this.

'Maybe not,' Long spoke with his head still lowered. 'But —'

'In fact,' C.J. went on, 'you only came *back* to the Reservation after your painting business in Los Angeles went bankrupt. Isn't that right?'

'So?' This time the Indian looked directly at her, with black defiance.

'So you returned to a place where you could feel safe,' C.J. went on, relentlessly. 'And you're sitting here today looking to get custody – *not* so you can pass on your *hopes and dreams*, but rather your *fears*. Your fear and hatred for the white world, Mr Long.'

The Indian stared at her with blank fury. 'You don't know the first thing about me,' he said in a soft, controlled voice.

'I know you're lying to this court,' said C.J.

'*Objection!*' cried Wauneka.

Judge Gainser leaned forward and said sternly, 'Why do you call this man a liar, Mr Lamb?'

'Because what he says isn't true, Your Honour,' she said calmly; and turned back to the man on the stand. 'But, Mr Long, it is true that when you married my client, you told

115

her you wanted *opportunities* for your son – chances that you never had growing up on the Reservation?'

'I also told her I was mistaken,' the Indian said, looking down again.

'Mr Long,' she said, 'let me show you a picture – a picture *you yourself* drew for my client.' She stepped forward and handed a sheet of paper to the man on the stand. 'Do you remember this?'

He stood and reluctantly unfolded it. 'Yes,' he said slowly.

'Did you draw those coyotes, and owls around it?' she asked. There was no reply.

'Let me see that,' Judge Gainser said.

She took the paper back from James Long and handed it up to the old man who sat inspecting it for a moment, frowning at first, then looking alarmed. 'Did you draw this?' he said at last, to the Indian.

James Long hung his head. 'I'm sorry, Your Honour.'

The Judge said something rapidly in Navajo; and the Indian on the stand nodded, staring glumly at his feet.

'For the record,' said C.J., 'tell us the symbolism of the coyotes and owls.'

Without lifting his head, Long said, 'They represent illness and bad luck.'

'*And death*,' said C.J. 'This picture means that, in your opinion, the Navajo Reservation is dying. Isn't that right, Mr Long?'

'It means,' Long said, lifting his head, 'that the Navajo Reservation *will* die, if it loses its children.'

Judge Gainser interrupted him. 'Why did you draw these omens around our land, Mr Long?'

The Indian turned, 'Because I believed our Nation would

116

fall to the oppression of the White Man. I am here today, trying to fight that oppression.'

'How ambitious!' C.J. said, with cruel irony. 'And here *I* am, just fighting for a little boy and his mother.'

'Objection,' said Wauneka.

'I have nothing further,' C.J. said, and sat down to a heavy silence.

*

The atmosphere that night in Victor Sifuentes' office was grim but business-like. Jonathan Rollins was in the client's chair, sitting next to Sifuentes – and at some distance from Assistant District Attorney Bill Graphia.

With them was a fourth man – District Attorney Mike Rogoff. A thick-set, handsome man with crimped grey hair and the hard, shrewd eyes of a political in-fighter, he was an old contact of Leland McKenzie – Leland was too fastidious to number the D.A. as a *friend* – who was coming up for re-election.

McKenzie guessed that a well-publicised case involving police brutality on a member of L.A.'s legal fraternity – and a possible race angle thrown in – could be just what District Attorney Rogoff needed for his campaign.

Sifuentes sat with his fingertips pressed together, speaking with quiet urgency. 'All right, now listen. This is the situation. Upon a closer look at the events' – he paused, looking at each of them in turn – 'we agree it's possible – *just possible* – that the officers were a little too reactive.'

'*Reactive?*' Rollins cried, with undisguised outrage.

Sifuentes held up his hand. 'Jonathan . . .?' he warned; then glanced at Graphia. 'So, what you do say, Bill?'

Graphia smiled portentously at Rollins, 'Nevertheless, you *did* resist, and a policeman got hurt. We can't dismiss. But we'll plea it out to a misdemeanour battery.'

Rollins looked furiously back at him, 'You're just looking for a conviction to insulate the Police Department from a civil suit. That's not going to happen.'

There was a leaden pause. Mike Rogoff now spoke, in his rich politician's voice, choosing his words with judicious care:

'Well then . . . as I see it, gentlemen, we got another problem. See, the grandmother who was raped' – he looked Rollins carefully in the eye – 'we showed her your picture – along with others, of course – and while she didn't conclusively I.D. you as the rapist – well, she couldn't rule you out, either.'

'Hey, what the hell is this?' Sifuentes cried, starting forward in his chair; while Jonathan Rollins just sat with a look of shock and growing terror on his face. Assaulting a member of the unloved L.A.P.D. was one thing – raping a senior citizen was in another league altogether. It was a nightmare.

Rogoff had glanced at Rollins, and now said quickly, to Sifuentes, 'Just a minute – I'm not saying I suspect him – at least, not on what I've seen so far . . .' He turned to Rollins, 'But you were in the area of the rape *at the time of the rape*. The victim's fingered you as a *possible*. And . . .'

Rollins exploded with rage. 'You bastards! You won't get away with this!'

Graphia came in smoothly. 'We're not accusing you, Mr Rollins – we're just trying to apprise you of all the circumstances.'

It was Sifuentes' turn to get angry. 'Get to the bottom line, Bill,' he said. 'What the hell is your message?'

Rogoff broke in, addressing Rollins direct:

'Get rid of this. The fact that she said it could be you . . .' – he began shaking his head – 'well, the officers will be screaming that as loud as they can, if they're ever forced to defend themselves. Take the plea – and the book on this gets closed. Reject the plea' – he shrugged and stood up – 'everything stays open-ended. There's your message.'

Rogoff and Graphia began to leave. Jonathan Rollins watched them, open-mouthed. '*Sonsofbitches*,' he murmured, as the door closed behind them.

Sifuentes said nothing. There was nothing more to say. The meeting was over.

*

'In addition to being a Doctor of Psychology,' the witness said, 'I'm also a Professor of Anthropology.'

'And you're a half-breed, Doctor Landale,' Wauneka said, with no trace of criticism.

'Yes, I am. So, I can tell you personally, as well as professionally, that raising Indian children in white families *does not work*.'

'Why, Doctor?'

'Because,' said the man on the stand, 'they're brought up white, with absolutely no sense of their Indian culture.'

'What's so wrong with that?' said Wauneka.

'Well, when they hit adolescence, they run head-first into a society that tells them they're *not* white. And since they have no Indian heritage to fall back on, they virtually become non-persons. This is extremely destructive.'

Judge Gainser interrupted, 'But, Doctor, what if Ms Long were careful to make Joshua *aware* of his culture?'

Dr Landale paused. 'Well,' he said thoughtfully, 'that's a very nice idea – but the reality is, if you assimilate this young man into a totally white environment . . . well, he's going to grow up with a white social identity – no matter what Ms Long does. And there's one other thing . . .'

'What's that?' Wauneka said eagerly.

'It is in any child's interest to see his race preserved. Indians are facing extinction. And every time you take an Indian child off the Reservation and assimilate him into white society, you're fostering cultural genocide. It's certainly not in Joshua's best interest to see his people wiped out.'

'Thank you, Dr Landale. That's all.'

Wauneka sat down, and C.J. rose in his place.

'You never examined this particular child,' she began, 'to make a determination which parent he'd be better off with – did you, Doctor?'

'No, I didn't.'

C.J. smiled. 'And, Doctor, what would happen to a boy's ability to bond and trust, should he be taken away from his mother?'

Doctor Landale hesitated. 'It could be compromised,' he said at last.

'*Compromised*,' C.J. repeated, with emphasis. 'And the damage could be irreparable, couldn't it?'

'A separation for a child of more than six months old rarely causes long-term harm.'

'But it *could*?' she pressed him.

'Severing his relationship with the Tribe could be just as devastating,' Dr Landale replied firmly.

C.J. nodded. 'Doctor Landale, what's the leading cause of death on the Reservation?'

There was silence: then Landale answered, in a small, reluctant voice, 'Alcoholism.'

'And what's the life-expectancy of an Indian male on this Reservation?' she asked.

'It's about forty-five years.'

'Did you factor this into your consideration of Joshua's best interests?'

The witness was looking very uncomfortable now. 'Medically, the Indians are probably not as advanced – that's true. But —'

'What about education?' C.J. persisted. 'What about unemployment? What about the fact that half the Indian population lives *below* the poverty-line?'

'You're raising the subjective standards of the White Man,' Dr Landale said defensively.

'I'm talking about the threat of hunger – the threat of poverty – of illiteracy, and of death being greater in the Indian world than it is in Western society. Are those subjective standards to you, Dr Landale?'

'My opinion,' he said awkwardly, 'is that this child is better off in the Indian community.'

'Yes, your opinion is very clear,' said C.J.; she paused. 'Where do *you* live, Dr Landale?'

'Objection!' cried Wauneka.

Judge Gainser held up his hand. 'No, I'd like to hear the answer. Where do you live?' he repeated, to the witness.

Dr Landale looked at the floor. 'Phoenix,' he said, defeated.

'Thank you,' C.J. said. 'I have nothing further.'

Chapter Fourteen

The next meeting to try and save Jonathan Rollins' skin was a full council of war. Besides Rollins himself, Kuzak, Sifuentes, Grace Van Owen and Tommy Mullaney were all present, in Kuzak's office. For with a rape charge pending, it wasn't just Rollins' hide that was on the line. The very name and reputation of McKenzie Brackman and Partners was at stake.

Kuzak, because they were meeting on his territory, had taken the chair. His brow was furrowed, his hands fidgeted in his lap, as he strove, like the rest of them, to see a way out of this mess. In the present climate of Political Correctness in California, a reputable law firm might easily beat a sordid case of racial assault on one of its members by a rogue cop. But the rape of a sixty-year-old grandmother was something different.

'There's got to be *something* we can do,' Kuzak said at last. He turned to Sifuentes. 'Did they say *anything* we could go public with?'

Sifuentes said gloomily, 'It was scripted, Mike. They were careful to paint the threat without crossing the line of extortion.'

Tommy Mullaney shifted back in his chair. 'But the message was there,' he drawled. 'If Jonathan fights, they put it out he's a rape suspect.'

A grim silence followed. Jonathan Rollins sat very still, not moving a muscle. Kuzak spoke at last, 'I hate to give in to this kind of crap' – he avoided meeting Rollins' eye as he said this – 'but I don't know what else to do.'

This time Rollins came to life. 'I'm not pleading out. I can't, Michael! I make that deal – then those two cops walk away heads high, totally vindicated.'

Grace Van Owen came in here, 'But if you don't plea . . .' – she shook her head despairingly – 'God, Jonathan, the stain of that woman I.D.ing you, it —'

'She didn't I.D. me,' Rollins said flatly.

'As a *possible*, she did. I don't care how inconclusive or tainted the make was' – Grace spoke with her usual grim, professional detachment – 'all they have to do is say there's evidence against you, but insufficient to prosecute. Your career will be dead for ever – not to mention your reputation.'

Rollins sat vigorously shaking his head. 'I can't take a plea here. I can't! I'd never be able to live with myself.' He looked desperately at Sifuentes. 'Victor, you have to know what I'm saying!'

Sifuentes looked gravely at him, 'I know exactly what you're saying, Jonathan. But I don't know what to tell you. If we fight' – his elegant hands spread in an empty, hopeless gesture – 'you just get hurt worse.'

For a moment Rollins stared back at him; then, with a faint look of disgust, slammed his chair back, stood up and walked out of the room.

In the silence that followed, Kuzak smacked both hands

on the desk and said, 'C'mon, for God's sake, we're all good lawyers here. We *have* to be able to come up with something? We can't just let Jonathan die on the vine . . .'

*

'Hi – sweetheart!' Tommy Mullaney stood in the doorway of A.D.A. Clemmons' office in the District Attorney's Building, smiling his roguish hangdog smile that seemed to be telling the whole world, *Yeah, I'm a tired old legal back, but if you get to know me better, you'll get to love me, too . . .!*

Ms Zoey Clemmons – formerly Mrs Zoey Mullaney – looked up from her desk and smiled back: a genuine, happy, surprised smile, for she was also pleased to see Tommy – even if some of the memories, if she bothered to dredge them up, were still a bit raw.

'Baby!' she cried.

Tommy advanced and folded her in a close, warm hug, then stood back and inspected her. 'Wow – you're gorgeous!' He meant it, too. For Zoey Clemmons was truly, dazzlingly pretty – but in a nice, open, friendly way – none of that hard Hollywood guile and *ingenue* cuteness that says, Aren't-I-just-lovely and go-to-hell! all in one breath. Zoey might be a tough professional attorney in the D.A.'s Office, but she was also that rare thing in L.A.: a decent, honest girl with a genuinely good face – soft, loose blonde hair and full lips, all concealing a first-class legal mind. Tommy adored her, still.

'C'mon in!' she went on, still smiling, then paused. 'How much?' she added, as though addressing a wilful child.

'No,' he said, shaking his head, 'I don't need money this

124

time – promise' – and he gave her the two-fingered salute, Indian-style.

Zoey gave a mock shudder. 'Oh God – last time you showed up unexpected, and not wanting money, you proposed! Please, Tommy – let me write you a cheque . . .'

He leaned close to her, no longer smiling. 'I need a favour, kid. A big one.'

'Uh-oh!' – she threw up her hands – 'I don't like the tone. So serious . . .'

'Yeah.' Mullaney lowered his head, speaking out of the side of his mouth. 'Name of Jonathan Rollins mean anything?'

She straightened up, beginning to frown. 'C'mon Tommy. The whole Department knows about that one.'

'He works in my firm,' Mullaney said. 'And he's a friend, Zoey. You know what's going down?'

She gave a faint shrug. 'I hear some things' – but her tone was evasive, unsettled.

'He's innocent,' Mullaney said. 'And you know that, too – don't ya?' He stood back, giving her his best level, honest-to-God expression. 'Look, honey – I don't mean to get you into any kinda trouble. But your people here are making him take a fall here for something he didn't do. And that kinda stuff don't sit with you too good – we both know that.'

Zoey stiffened. 'What do you want, Tommy?'

'I want you to get involved.' His voice was a slow, soft, urgent drawl. 'If you can make it go away, I want you to make it go away.'

She gave him an upward, plaintive look from under her blonde eyelashes. 'I can't help you on this one. Sorry, baby. I can't.'

125

Mullaney hadn't moved, his eyes still fixed on hers. She flinched. 'Look,' she went on, sounding slightly desperate. 'It goes beyond the Department protecting a couple of reckless cops. This is bigger – believe me.'

'How much bigger?'

She hesitated only a second. 'The buzz in the office is that Rogoff owes the police some serious political payback. And – well, they've come collecting on this one. On the Rollins case.'

Mullaney gave a deep sigh and straightened up across the desk. 'Dig it up for me, Zoey. You gotta give me something I can use —'

'I haven't got anything you can use!' she broke in. 'You can't win this, Tommy. Don't try to be a hero!'

'The kid *needs* a hero!' he shouted back. 'I'm sorry, Zoey – I know I got no right putting you in the middle here . . . But this thing – it's a little hard to walk away from.'

She lowered her eyes. 'I wish I could help,' she murmured. 'I do.'

'Yeah,' Mullaney said meanly. 'Me too!' He gave a last hard look, then swung round and left the room.

Zoey didn't even watch him leave. She sat staring at the desk-top in front of her; then, as she heard the door snap shut behind him, she reached for the phone.

'Cindy? Get me the Brian Chisolm File. All of it. Right now . . .'

*

Janice Long stood limp and dejected, her long black hair hanging down below her shoulders, and answered C.J.'s

126

question, in a low, quavering voice that tiptoed on the brink of tears.

'I don't doubt Jim's ability to be a good father,' she said. 'And I know he loves his son very much. But I've taken care of Joshua all his life. I've been with him every day. I can't —' She struggled to control herself, biting back the tears. 'He should be with me.'

'I think the fear is,' C.J. said gently, 'if Joshua lives with you, he'll miss out on his Indian culture.'

The woman on the stand gave her a forlorn look. 'I don't intend to make him forget he's an Indian,' she said feebly. 'Look, I can't sit here and defend American society. And maybe . . . maybe I can't give him some of the things you talk about – some of the Indian ways,' she added, looking forlornly round the small, crowded Navajo Courtroom; but the rows of silent Indian faces offered no comfort.

'I'm his mother,' she went on, 'I'm the only one who can give him that. Whatever a little boy may need growing up in *any* culture or society . . . my God! – he has to have his mother.'

'Thank you, Ms Long.' She nodded. 'I have nothing further.'

When she'd returned to her chair, Wauneka rose, faced Janice Long, and said, without ceremony, 'You, yourself rejected the Indian way of life, didn't you, Ms Long?'

She looked back at the well-dressed Indian attorney and a spark of defiance showed in her tired eyes. 'I rejected living on a Reservation – yes, I did.'

Wauneka paused, then said casually, 'What's a Healing-way, Ms Long?'

There was a tense pause. Janice frowned. 'I'm not sure. It's Navajo, I know.'

127

'It's a name of an Indian ceremony,' said Wauneka. 'What's a Flintway?'

C.J. was on her feet: 'Objection.'

Wauneka cut in smoothly, 'Your Honour, the witness suggests she won't cause the child to abandon his heritage. When it's clear that she herself doesn't know anything about how we live.'

This suddenly brought Janice Long to the boil. 'Let me tell you how I lived on your Reservation, Mr Wauneka. I had to chop wood and lug water every day.'

'Move to strike,' said Wauneka.

The Judge leaned towards Janice. 'No. I weant to hear her answer.'

When she spoke, Janice Long's voice had a certain dull passion. 'I was ostracized because I couldn't herd sheep or speak Navajo. I had to live in a hogan without electricity. Without running water. And, as a white person, I was the enemy – and none of you can deny that. I was treated as an outsider.'

She paused, glaring at the smart-suited Indian attorney: 'If I rejected *you*, Mr Wauneka, it's because you rejected me first. So don't you stand there calling me a bigot.' She sucked in her breath; and her next words were hurled across the little Courtroom with a peculiar, deadly passion, *'Because all of you are racists!'* she cried.

There was no reaction in the room whatsoever. Slowly, C.J. rose to her feet. 'Janice —' she began.

'No – I want to say this.' There was colour in the girl's cheeks now, her eyes glistening with tears. 'My son is Indian. I want him to know that – and I want him to be proud of that. But more than anything else' – her voice choked, stumbled, picked up again – 'more than anything else, I want to teach him that people are people are people. *Race doesn't matter.*' Her voice dropped almost to a whisper, 'At least, not to me.'

'Probably,' Wauneka said spitefully, 'because *your* race isn't the one being wiped out.'

'Objection,' said C.J.

Judge Gainser looked hard at the witness. 'Are you telling us – your son's Indian race doesn't matter?'

Janice Long hesitated. 'It . . . it matters. But what matters more is that I'm that boy's mother.' She lifted her head and looked the old Judge straight in the eye. 'I gave birth to that little boy. And he shouldn't lose me – just because I'm white.'

*

It was very hot in the little Courtroom, as David Wauneka delivered his closing argument. There was nothing Indian about it: his speech was fluent and persuasive, with all the scientific rhetoric and hyperbole of an expensively trained American city lawyer.

'I don't think there's much doubt that both parents love Joshua very much. But under the Indian Child Welfare Fact – the *Federal Law*, as passed by the United States Congress – you also have to take into account what's best for the Tribe.' He paused. His audience sat impassive. Janice Long was crying.

'The Indian culture,' Wauneka went on, 'is faced with genocide. Thirty percent of our children are taken away, ninety percent of those going to white families who cause these children to abandon their heritage. You heard Janice Long. She rejects us. How can any child raised under her influence' – he threw a cruel glance at Janice Long – 'grow to love or even *respect* what we are.'

He paused again, balancing perilously on the edge of self-pity. 'It's a desperate thing, I suppose,' he went on, as though reflecting to himself, 'to cling to children as a means of propagating a race. But genocide is a desperate thing.' He turned again to Janice Long, 'I understand your pain, ma'am, I only hope that one day you will come to understand ours.' He bowed his head to Judge Gainser and returned to his chair in silence.

*

C.J.'s clean, clipped English vowels were as foreign here as the tomahawk would have been in her native Surrey:

'They call America a melting pot. A place where all cultures come together as one. The trouble is – with the American Indian – we're trying to melt the entire race. We took your land. "Assimilated" your people, as we politely put it.' She gave a loose, ironic gesture, letting her hand drop to her side:

'Well, like Mr Wauneka said,' she went on, 'your Tribe is being eroded away. It should stop.' She paused, looking towards Janice Long, 'but this isn't the way. You cannot attempt to serve your heritage – at the expense of a two-year-old-boy. And that's what they're asking you to do. He has lived every day of his life with her. When he cries, *she's* the one he runs to. When he's happy *she's* the one he wants to share his joy with. This woman *is* that boy's life. There is nobody he trusts more. Nobody he loves more.' She paused again, this time meeting Judge Gainser's eye and holding it:

'He lives in Los Angeles. Let him go home, Judge. Let him go home with his mother.'

The old man lowered his eyes. For a long time he said nothing. The only sound in the Courtroom was Janice Long's sobbing.

*

'This is your last chance, Jonathan,' Victor Sifuentes said. 'You sure you want to go through with it?'

Rollins gave a weary shrug. 'Do I have any other choice?'

The Criminal Court was full of busy lawyers and officials, gathered in groups or scurrying about, completing a motions session before the main work of the Court began. As Sifuentes finished speaking to Rollins, he glimpsed the bulky grey figure of District Attorney Rogoff appear quietly at the back of the Courtroom. What had brought him here this morning? Sifuentes wondered: and who's side was he on . . .?

From the well of the Court, the Clerk was calling out: 'Case Number 93571 – People versus Jonathan Rollins . . .'

As Sifuentes and Rollins took their seats, Bill Graphia stepped forward, addressing Judge Shubov: 'Your Honour, the parties are prepared to offer a plea.'

There was a stirring from the Press benches, which were packed. Sifuentes and his client waited, both stiff with anticipation.

'All assault counts dropped,' A.D.A. Graphia went on, 'Mr Rollins agrees to plead guilty to misdemeanour battery on the resist. Joint recommendation for sixty days probation.'

Judge Shubov nodded. 'Defence so agrees?'

Before Sifuentes could answer, there came a cry from the well of the Court. Zoey Clemmons was hurrying down the aisle, between the rows of eager reporters. 'Your Honour . . .!' she cried breathlessly, 'Zoey Clemmons – Assistant District Attorney. If I may be heard . . .!'

There was a stirring, murmuring sound across the packed benches in the Courtroom. Every head was turned, all eyes fixed on Zoey – her striking prettiness emphasised by a bright canary-yellow suit.

'Approach,' ordered Judge Shubov.

'Your Honour,' Zoey called, 'I have information which draws into question the legality of this prosecution . . .'

Bill Graphia was half out of his chair, standing close to her now. 'What are you doing?' he called anxiously.

'Shut up, Billy!' she whispered.

At the back of the Court, Rogoff was stirring uneasily, as Judge Shubov growled down at them, 'What's going on?'

Zoey Clemmons had halted, catching her breath. 'Your Honour, several months ago the District Attorney's Office – which I represent – prosecuted a police officer by the name of Brian Chisolm, who was charged with the fatal shooting of a black teenager. Ironically, it was the defendant here today – Mr Rollins, himself – who defended this officer.'

Judge Shubov nodded. 'I remember. So what?'

'Your Honour' – Zoey could barely conceal her excitement – 'because of the racial tension surrounding this event, Mr Rogoff was faced with a tremendous backlash, at just the time he needed the Black vote to win his re-election.'

A loud murmur began to swell across the Courtroom, so that Zoey had to raise her voice to make herself heard. 'It is widely believed within the Department,' she went on, almost shouting, 'that Mr Rogoff originally prosecuted

132

Brian Chisolm for the sole purpose of appeasing his black constituency – in order to secure that re-election . . .!'

Through the uproar on the Court floor, District Attorney Rogoff was already thrusting his way forward, elbowing aside the excited crowds on the Press benches. 'That's a bare-faced lie!' he shouted.

'Mr Rogoff, be quiet!' the Judge replied, with an unexpected lack of reverence.

Zoey Clemmons, trying to disregard this intervention from her boss, pressed on with remorseless courage:

'Further, upon information and belief, Police Chief Kevin Vance was prepared to publicly condemn Mr Rogoff for what *he* believed to be the political sacrifice of one of his officers. Chief Vance and Mike Rogoff then struck a deal whereby the Chief would agree to stay quiet on the Chisolm issue.'

At the defendant's table, Rollins glanced at Sifuentes. 'Is this possible?' he whispered.

Sifuentes grinned, 'Why not? This is L.A. . . .'

Zoey's voice cut loudly across the noise of the Courtroom. 'In Exchange,' she cried, 'District Attorney Rogoff promised to back the Police Department at every turn in future. Vance is sticking Rogoff for the payback in this case!' she shouted conclusively.

Graphia was on his feet now, the tension seeping through his suave exterior. 'Your Honour, this isn't about politics!' he protested; he sounded close to panic. 'The fact is – Mr Rollins committed a crime.'

'Nobody believes Mr Rollins is a criminal,' Zoey Clemmons shouted back. 'This is about ass-covering. Furthermore, Your Honour' – and she turned, indicating an increasingly perplexed Jonathan Rollins – 'it's widely believed within the Department that Mr Rollins has been blackmailed into accepting today's plea.'

Judge Shubov's eyebrows jerked up a full inch, 'Go on.'

'If Rollins doesn't capitulate,' Zoey said, 'the Department is prepared to cite him as a possible rape suspect – despite a total absence of good faith and any real belief that he committed such a crime.'

The Judge now turned and looked hard at Sifuentes, 'Did they hang rape over your guy's head?'

Sifuentes nodded. 'Yes, Your Honour.'

Graphia jumped up. 'You can't prove any of this.'

Zoey turned contemptuously, 'Remember, I'm in that office, Billy. I know what goes on in there. Everybody knows what's going on.' She looked at the Judge, with an emphatic gesture towards Graphia:

'This man is one of our top A.D.A.s, Judge. Why would he be assigned to a simple felony? Why is District Attorney, Mike Rogoff, monitoring this case himself? Why is he in this room for a plea bargain?'

There was a heavy pause. Judge Shubov sat, slowly scratching his ear. Then he nodded thoughtfully down at Zoey Clemmons. 'I guess I could ask,' he said finally, 'why *you* are here, ma'am?'

Zoey spoke defiantly, 'I'm coming forward as an Officer of the Court, to prevent what I believe to be a gross violation of the judicial process. District Attorney Mike Rogoff has abused his power. Jonathan Rollins is an innocent man. I'm here in what could be my last act as an A.D.A., asking the Court to remedy an extremely unjust situation. Thank you.'

To a rising roar of excitement and applause, she swung and headed down the aisle and out of the Courtroom.

When the hubbub had died down, Graphia gave a dismissive shrug. 'I don't know where *that* came from, but —' he began.

'Shut up,' growled Judge Shubov. He looked down at Mike Rogoff, 'Don't worry, Mr Rogoff – I only believe every word,' he said, with savage irony. 'A warrant is hereby issued for your arrest for the obstruction of justice.'

Rogoff's neck swelled, his face turned puce. 'You have no authority to do that!' he bellowed.

'Watch me,' Judge Shubov replied triumphantly. 'The Court Officers will take Mr Rogoff into custody. Mr Graphia, be thankful I don't lock you up as well!' he added, and turned to the defendant's table. 'The complaint against Jonathan Rollins is hereby dismissed on all counts,' he ordered.

'This is a complete farce!' Rogoff yelled at Shubov. 'You're right out of order . . .!'

This time the Judge had had enough. 'Put that man in lock-up now!' he called to the Court Officials. 'And don't forget to read him his rights!' he added, without irony.

Below him, Rollins and Sifuentes had relaxed in happy disbelief.

Chapter Fifteen

The little Tribal Courtroom at Window Rock was packed and airless, full of that strange dry Indian smell that is somewhere between old sweat and the sweet scent of burnt mesquite wood.

James and Janice Long were standing in the front row, before the former Medicine Man, Judge Gainser, and separated by their respective attorneys, David Wauneka and C.J. Lamb. These last two looking like a couple of glamorous models, showing off the latest City fashions against a strikingly 'ethnic' background.

If the contrast was noticed by Judge Gainser, he showed no sign of it; instead, he nodded to the four in front of him. 'Parties approach. Lawyers too, please.

As they took up their positions in front of him – James Long and Wauneka, with their eyes dutifully lowered – he began to deliver his judgement, in a slow, almost folksy monotone, against the same packed stillness of the Courtroom:

'As a Navajo, I bring to the bench my subjective belief – that the White Man is a nemesis who destroys the land and who eventually will bring ruin to himself. I also believe that since Congress has trusted me to *protect* the Tribe, I am authorised to fight the White Man's dominance. One of the most effective ways I can do that is to stop him from taking our children. Without the child to pass on our philosophies, our religions, our *ways* – our ways die. The genocide, Mr Wauneka speaks of – we've all seen it happen. We all desperately want to stop it.'

He paused, his eyes on the desk before him; and the silence in the little room was so intense they could hear a fly buzzing and bumping gently against the window frame. The Indians along the benches sat like carved wooden figures, their black eyes cast down on the floor in front of them. Only C.J. Lamb and her client, Janice Long, stood erect, watching the Judge intently.

The old man continued, in the same flat gentle voice, almost as though he were talking to himself:

'But even *more* steeped in our tradition, is the *protection* of the child's relationship with his mother. And without any evidence that this mother is unfit to raise her son, I'm not going to strip her of custody.

James Long broke in softly, without raising his head, 'Your Honour, please . . .'

Without looking at him, Judge Gainser replied, 'I would love nothing better than to give in to my own prejudices and to award him to you, Mr Long.' He paused, then glanced up at the Navajo Court Official. 'Bring in the boy, please.'

As the official went out, the Judge looked, this time, straight at James Long. 'But a rejection of Indian life, unfortunately, is not grounds enough.' His flat black stare moved on to Janice Long:

'Ms Long, just as you prayed I would not overlook the

137

truth that this child is your son, I pray that *you* not overlook the other truth – that he is a Navajo.'

He looked up, and there was a stir from the crowded benches, as the door opened again and the Court official reappeared, leading the tiny figure of Joshua Long. The child looked bewildered, more than frightened. For a moment he didn't seem to notice his mother and father, among all these silent grown-up faces.

Judge Gainser spoke with quiet, supreme dignity. 'The order of the California Superior Court is upheld. Give the boy to Ms Long.'

James Long took a sudden step forward. For the first time his voice, his whole being, gave vent to a terrible inner passion, 'Please. Let me hold him, first.'

Judge Gainser nodded, and the Court official led the little boy towards his father. James Long bent down, held the child by the arms in his big brown hands and began to murmur to him, in a curious mixture of Navajo and English, 'I love you, son. You be a good boy. Don't forget your father.' Then, in a last burst of emotion: '*Don't forget your people.*'

He kissed his son, then slowly straightened up, his face again totally without expression, and passed the child to his mother.

When it was all over, C.J. leant over and kissed Janice Long on both cheeks. Janice was crying, with a mixture of joy and unbearable relief.

'Next case,' said Judge Gainser.

*

It was late; Zoey Clemmons' office was quiet and dim, lit

only by a desk lamp and the flickering glow of a twenty-four-inch TV screen in a wall-to-wall bookcase lined with leather-bound volumes of Federal Law.

Zoey lay back on a reclining leather chair, her shoes on the floor, a cigarette between her fingers. She felt limp, drained, like a ship-wrecked sailor cast up on a dark and lonely beach. Her future, and that of her boss, was being signalled by a tight-lipped anchorman now reading the autocue on the TV:

'. . . *District Attorney Mike Rogoff, meanwhile, is steadfastly denying all allegations. Assistant District Attorney Mark Sheer will become acting D.A. for the duration of the investigation . . .*'

Zoey reached for the remote control and flicked the screen into darkness. She took a deep breath, steadied her hand, and was just taking a pull on her cigarette when there came a quiet knock at the door. She murmured something, too tired to move, and watched Tommy Mullaney and Jonathan Rollins come in.

Mullaney gave his crinkle-eyed smile. 'Hi.'

'Hi,' she said, in barely a whisper.

Mullaney took a step forward, while Rollins hung back near the door, almost invisible in the darkness. 'Got somebody here – wanted to meet ya,' Mullaney said, quiet and casual.

Zoey turned her head, still not moving from the chair, and saw Jonathan Rollins step tentatively forward into the circle of light from the desk lamp. He seemed embarrassed.

Zoey gave him a tired smile. 'I'm sorry you had to go through such an ordeal, Mr Rollins.'

Rollins' voice, when he managed to speak, was tight with

humility, 'I don't know how I can ever repay you, Ms Clemmons.'

'*Zoey*,' she said, 'call me Zoey.'

'Zoey,' Rollins repeated, with the tiniest glint of a smile. 'Nobody ever went out on a limb for me as much as you did today. And you don't even know me,' he added, his voice straining with emotion.

Zoey gave an exhausted shrug and gestured with her cigarette towards her former husband: 'It's him. He makes me do crazy things – that's why I had to leave him . . .'

'Yeah, well . . .' Rollins began, stammering, 'I owe him, too.' He hesitated, glancing at them both and swallowing hard. He seemed to be groping for the words and not finding them. 'Yes – well . . . Thank you. Thank you . . .'

Mullaney turned to him. 'Gimme a minute, would ya, Jonathan. We'll be right out.'

'Sure. Sure.' Glad to conceal his tongue-tied embarrassment, Rollins nodded and slipped quietly out of the room.

Mullaney turned and gave his former wife a funny, slack-jawed grin. 'You gonna be okay here?' His tone was slow and easy-going, almost off-hand; he was still giving nothing away.

She sucked on her cigarette and smiled. 'It's a little scary, I guess. If Rogoff's really out, I'm okay. If he comes back into power, I go back into private practice. So far, I'd say it looks fifty-fifty.'

Mullaney seemed to hesitate. 'Y'know' – he watched her draw again on her cigarette and breathe out slowly, the smoke uncoiling in the lamplight like gentle sea mist – 'sometimes it's hard to believe you were such a God-awful wife. 'Cause you're still the greatest person I ever met.'

She sighed. 'Can I quote you on my resumé?'

'Sure.' He took a long stride towards her, bent down and gave her a close, warm hug.

Her voice had a strange hushed crack in it when she spoke: 'You're such a goddamned bad influence, Tommy . . .'

'I know,' he said, kneeling down beside her. 'I know.'

'While I'm still an Assistant D.A., I should have you locked up,' she said, as his mouth sank down against hers.

*

'All right people, busy days for everyone! Let's keep this short.' Douglas Brackman sat at the head of the table, rubbing his hands together. 'First up, on a *very* exciting note. I spoke last evening with Hendrick Shay, Estate Planning Counsel for Rikki Davis.'

'*The* Rikki Davis?' cried Ann Kelsey.

Brackman nodded. 'Yes – and for those of you who've been skipping Page One for the last few months – Ms Davis, along with her lover, is being charged with murdering her seventy-two-year-old husband.'

'The "Beverly Hills Hangers"?' Mullaney said, rousing himself in his chair.

'The very ones,' Brackman said. 'The young widow is apparently upset with her Defence Counsel. She wants to interview *us*.'

'Wow!' cried Markowitz, beaming round the table.

Mike Kuzak leant forward, 'I want that case, Douglas.'

'You've got it, Michael. Providing you can hook her. She's coming in this morning, at eleven.' He glanced round the table. 'Needless to say, this would be a public relations

141

home-run. It's probably the most talked-about murder case in the country.'

'I want to work on this, too,' Jonathan Rollins broke in.

The excitement was spreading. 'Let me second chair, Michael,' Abby said to Kuzak.

Ann Kelsey, meanwhile, sat hard-faced across the table. 'Why does Michael always get the big cases?' she grumbled. 'For once, I'd like a murder case – *maybe*,' she added, letting the bitterness show.

'Ann, you *never* want murder cases,' Kuzak said.

'I want *this* one,' she said fiercely.

'Well, you can't have it.'

'All right,' Brackman interrupted, raising his hand with pedagogic solemnity. 'There'll probably be work for everyone here – if we get the case. Michael, I might suggest bringing someone else in for the meeting with Ms Davis. Whatever it takes to snag her.' He paused.

'Next up, Jonathan' – he frowned at Rollins – 'are you still planning to proceed with your action against the police?'

'Yes, Douglas, I am.' Rollins was decisive but conciliatory. 'I'm not chasing the D.A.'s office, though – out of deference to Zoey Clemmons.'

Sifuentes glanced at Mullaney, 'How's she doing, Tommy?'

'Good,' Mullaney said. 'Rogoff's been suspended. Looks pretty good. He'll take the fall. Zoey's right back in the saddle with assignments.'

Brackman heard this and nodded judiciously: 'Glad to hear it.' Then added, with high pomposity, 'Be appraised, everyone – I'm out of the office Wednesday morning with some minor bunion surgery.' He slapped his folder shut. 'That's all, people. We're adjourned.'

Chapter Sixteen

Orin Baldwin was a large man, with the coarse, wide-pored complexion of lightly toasted bread, and the dry glittering eyes of a heavy drinker. He sat heavy and subdued, in his chair in the Witness Room of the Criminal Court, his eyes fixed on the Prosecutor, Zoey Clemmons.

At his side was his personal attorney, a local hot-shot called Brian Byrd, who was wearing a mohair suit the colour of burnished copper, black alligator shoes, and a chunky diamond ring on his pinky-finger, which he kept well-displayed throughout the interview.

Both men smelled of money, not necessarily of the clean variety. Zoey Clemmons disliked them both on sight – a spontaneous impression confirmed by the nature of the indictment before her.

'Cop to the rape,' she said briskly to Orin Baldwin, ignoring Byrd, 'I'll go with low term – and you'll be out in eighteen months.'

'That's ridiculous,' the big man growled.

Byrd laid a hand gently on his client's sleeve. 'Orin, please' – then, with an oily smile at Zoey, 'Misdemeanour battery – suspended.'

Zoey sat back and gave the attorney a slow sarcastic smile. 'He rapes a sixteen-year-old girl – and you expect him to walk on a misdemeanour?' she said, not bothering to keep the distaste out of her voice.

Orin Baldwin leaned forward in his chair. 'I didn't rape anybody. She got what she was looking for and —'

'Orin,' Byrd said softly, '*please*.'

Baldwin shrugged petulantly. 'If it hadn't been me, it would have been someone else —'

Byrd gave Zoey his smooth professional smile. 'As we've agreed, Ms Clemmons – any statements made in this room are in the context of a plea negotiation and therefore wholly inadmissible.'

Zoey countered his smile with a fierce, implacable stare. 'Did you contact the girl's mother and offer three hundred thousand dollars to drop this thing?' she asked.

The lawyer's smile didn't flicker. 'That offer anticipated a potential *civil* claim. It would be illegal, of course, for me to tamper with a *criminal* prosecution.'

Zoey nodded. 'Yeah – well, she got the impression that's *exactly* what you were doing.'

'She misunderstood,' Byrd said, with a slight edge this time.

Zoey looked at him. 'Now you just listen to me, Mr Byrd. If I get wind you're offering bribes – or doing *anything* to buy your way out of this – I'll bring you both up on obstruction of justice.'

'Don't threaten me, Ms Clemmons,' Byrd said, with honeyed menace.

Zoey didn't flinch. 'Stay away from the girl. Stay away from the mother. That's what I'm telling you, Byrd.'

Stung by this offensive familiarity, most of the sweetness

had gone from his lawyerly voice, as he snarled, 'Until they're represented by civil counsel – and thus far they're *not* – I'm entitled to approach them.'

'Go near them again,' Zoey said implacably, 'and I'm bringing charges.' She turned to Orin Baldwin, and this time let him see her full contempt, 'I don't care how many banks you own, or how many lawyers you hire, Mr Baldwin. I'll screw up your life.'

The big man just stared morosely back at her.

Byrd said, 'You'll never make rape *or* statutory rape' – all the professional charm had worn off and he was speaking now in the bare-knuckle tones of a street-fighter – 'and after we beat the girl up in the criminal case – and make no mistake, I *will* get her – we'll be bringing a civil libel case against her. Even if we don't win, we'll bankrupt them in legal bills. Tell your people *that*, Ms Clemmons! Then ask them if they *really* want to go forward with this.' He paused, smiling like a razor, 'Now – if you'll excuse us.'

Zoey Clemmons said nothing, as she watched them both march out of the room.

*

Mike Kuzak and Tommy Mullaney had been stunned by their visitor's appearance. Rikki Davis was in her late twenties, shaped like a dream – even by Californian standards. Long hair, the colour of ripe peaches, reaching down to her slim shoulders; the curves of her body modestly contained in a tailored suit of yellow slub-silk; and the kind of legs that Hollywood insure for ten million dollars.

She was sitting in Kuzak's office, her long slim legs

crossed and showing several inches of honey-coloured skin above the knee.

'My last lawyer suggested I plead out,' she said, speaking in a soft formal voice, without any hint that her life or liberty might hang on this meeting. 'That means either he *thinks* I'm guilty, or he doesn't think he can win. Either way, a switch seems in order.'

'John Fryar's a pretty sharp defence attorney,' Mullaney said, doubtfully. Rikki Davis gave him a flat stare. 'If he's telling me to admit to a crime I didn't commit, Mr Mullaney, he's not sharp enough.'

Mullaney paused, scratching his sandy chin. 'From what I gather in the newspapers, you have a tough case,' he drawled.

Rikki Davis eyed him suspiciously. 'What exactly have you gathered, Mr Mullaney?'

He went on fingering his chin. 'Your husband was found dead a week after he decided to divorce you.' He gave her a quizzical smile. 'A divorce would have cut you off at the knees with a pre-nup, while his *death*, on the other hand, leaves you twenty-six million as the grieving widow. You also had a lover. They found his prints, along with yours, on the cord used to hang your husband. That's pretty much it.'

'Those prints,' she said indignantly, 'were on the beam – not the cord – and they got there when we *discovered* him and tried to cut him down. We didn't hang him.'

'Then who did?' Kuzak said.

'I think maybe he hung *himself*.' She looked away, as she added, 'He was depressed.'

'About what?' said Kuzak.

She frowned. 'A month ago he was diagnosed with inoperable liver cancer. I know that's not much to go on.

But I didn't murder my husband. I didn't participate in any *conspiracy* to murder him. And I need a lawyer who can help me prove that.'

'I'll need all the files from John Fryar's office,' Kuzak said. 'Today. I also want you to take a lie-detector test.'

She opened her eyes wide, 'Why?'

'Because you evidently want a lawyer who believes in your innocence. I'm not there yet. Are you, Tommy?' he added, turning.

'Nope,' Mullaney said, watching the girl with his lazy grey eyes.

Kuzak looked at her doubtfully. 'Why don't you think it over?' he said, after a pause.

She shook her head. 'No. You're hired. Set up the polygraph and let me know.' Her deep-flecked eyes held Kuzak's for a moment; then she unfolded her legs and stood up. 'Nice to meet you both,' she said, and left the room.

Mullaney glanced across at his partner. 'Nice touch with the lie detector, Mike.'

Kuzak shrugged, 'I figured that would get her attention.'

'I want in on this case, Michael. As much as possible.'

'Oh, don't worry, Tommy. I got big plans for you.'

'Good. 'Cause this thing here – this is serious juice.'

They both smiled. This looked like being a useful morning's work.

*

Shirley Penn was a scraggy, forty-year-old blonde with the haggard eyes of a woman who didn't sleep well. With her, in Zoey Clemmons' office in the D.A.'s Building, was her daughter, Laurie – a plump, doe-eyed girl of sixteen, who sat nervously stroking her bare knee.

Zoey faced them both across her desk, addressing the mother. 'I certainly don't want you to back down. But I don't want to mislead you. If we prosecute, his lawyer's gonna do anything he can to destroy you. And his lawyer is great.'

'Does she have to testify?' Shirley Penn asked, in a small tired voice. 'I mean, with statutory rape, consent doesn't matter – right?'

Zoey nodded gravely. 'But we're also going with straight rape. On that one, consent *is* an issue.'

'Maybe we should drop that one,' the mother said feebly.

'That would be a mistake. Our best shot's on the straight count. With statutory rape, the only issue is age and he can argue mistaken belief that she looked old enough. If we go forward, we really should go with both counts.'

The daughter looked up at Zoey. 'Can you get him convicted?' she asked nervously. There was no hint of guile or evasion in her manner.

'I don't know, Laurie.'

The mother broke in, with sudden fierceness, 'No, I don't want her put through this.'

'Mom . . .' – the daughter looked at her, both defiant and beseeching.

'Honey,' Shirley Penn said, looking protectively at her daughter, 'you have no idea how hard it will be in there. And the likelihood is you'll lose. It'll be all for nothing.'

Laurie turned instead to Zoey; she sounded calm now, even resolute. 'What do *you* think?' she asked her.

'I want to prosecute,' Zoey said firmly. 'But your mother's right. There's a good chance we'll lose.'

149

There was a tense pause, as Laurie just sat and stared at Zoey. Zoey waited, her expression giving nothing away, determined to let the girl make up her own mind.

'I want to go through with it,' Laurie said at last. 'He raped me. How can I just let him get away with it?'

Zoey looked at her for a moment in silence. 'You understand,' she said, in the severe but gentle tones of an adult guiding a child, 'how tough – how strong you'll have to be in that witness chair?'

'I can do it. I'm ready to do it.'

Zoe Clemmons smiled. 'Then so am I.'

*

Laurie Penn looked very small on the stand, at the far end of the big, crowded Criminal Courtroom. Above her, Judge Douglas McGrath presided in silent majesty; while below them, at the Defence table, Orin Baldwin and his attorney, Byrd, sat like two well-dressed 'heavies', their anxiety concealed with an air of patient boredom. Neither of them looked at the girl while she gave her testimony; Baldwin's ugly head was down, as he busily scribbled notes on the table in front of him.

Zoey Clemmons asked Laurie, 'When did you first meet this group?'

'At the bar.' The girl's voice was quiet, diffident – but much less nervous than Zoey had feared. 'They were on a business trip or something,' Laurie went on, 'and he invited us up to his suite.'

'*He* being the defendant?' said Zoey.

'Yes.'

'How old are you, Laurie?'

'Sixteen.'

'What were you doing in a hotel bar having drinks?'

'I don't know.' She lowered her eyes. 'We were sitting at home – bored – and, I don't know. We just decided to go out.'

'Okay.' Zoey gave her a small smile of encouragement. 'But I want you to tell us exactly how you happened to go up to the defendant's suite.'

'Well – we were all having fun at the bar. There were two other men and a woman, besides Carol and m∴. And we talked about ordering room service and stuff up there. Carol and I just thought – well, we didn't think they were dangerous or anything.'

'Okay. So what happened after you got there?'

'Well' – a slightly coy, knowing tone had crept into the girl's voice – 'we all talked. We danced a little – there was a stereo. I was dancing with him – Orin.' She nodded vaguely down at the big man at the defendant's table, without looking directly at him; Orin Baldwin did not look at her.

'Did you like this?' Zoey asked her.

She shrugged. 'Sure. He seemed really cool. Even though he was older.'

'So what happened?'

'At about 12.30 Carol said she had to leave 'cause she had to be home by one. He said he'd drive me home, so . . .'

'You stayed,' said Zoey.

'Yes.'

'And what happened after your girlfriend left?'

'The other people left too, to go back to their rooms. He made another drink. There was one of those mini-bars in the room. Then we . . . we hugged. And we kissed.'

'You willingly kissed him?'

151

'Yes.'

'Then what?'

'Then um . . . we started kissing, heavier y'know, a lot and – then he began putting his hands on my breasts. I told him no, but – he kept telling me to relax. He pushed me on to the bed. I tried to get away but I couldn't. He kept saying, "*you know you want it* . . ." Then he pulled up my dress. I just screamed.'

'You screamed?'

'Yes. And I scratched him and tried to get out from under him but – I couldn't. He pinned me by my arms. He was too strong, I couldn't get him off. The next thing I know – he was pushing himself inside of me.'

'When you say he was pushing himself inside of you –'

'He was raping me. I tried to fight him. But I couldn't.'

'Okay.' Zoey paused. 'And Laurie – are you sure the defendant *knew* you didn't want intercourse?'

'Yes, he knew. I was screaming at him to stop. I was screaming for *help*. He knew.'

'But he wouldn't stop.'

'No.' Suddenly the girl's composure cracked, and she began to sob. 'No, he wouldn't stop.'

'Thank you. I have nothing further,' Zoey said, and returned to her seat. There was dead silence in the Court, broken only by the girl's sobbing.

Judge McGrath cleared his throat noisily and said, 'We'll take a short break – let the witness compose herself.'

*

The man operating the lie detector had the dry, scrubbed look of an embalmer's assistant. His face was utterly without expression, as he faced the gorgeous Rikki Davis across the desk in Kuzak's office. Her bolero jacket had been removed. She wore a sleeveless crepe shirt; her bare arms were hooked up to an ugly array of wires attached to what looked like a computer terminal.

Kuzak and Mullaney were watching carefully, as the polygraph operator intoned the questions, reading off a list prepared for him by Kuzak.

'You were married to your husband for three years?'

'Yes.'

'Did you love him?'

'Very much.'

'Did you know he was planning to divorce you?'

'No.'

'Mrs Davis – did you murder your husband?'

'No, I did not.'

'Did your lover, David Shaeffer, murder your husband?'

'No, he did not.'

'Do you know who hanged your husband?'

'No, I do not.'

'Thank you. That's all.' The operator looked up at Kuzak. 'We're done.' As he spoke, he was already unfastening the wires from Rikki Davis' arms, with the swift, dispassionate efficiency of a doctor.

Kuzak nodded to her, unsmiling. 'Wait here one second, Rikki. We'll be right back.'

He stood up and led the polygraph operator out to the office complex, followed by Tommy Mullaney. They both stepped just outside the closed door, and looked expectantly at the man. His face was expressionless, his voice detached, 'She's telling the truth.'

'You sure?' Mullaney said.

153

The man gave the faintest hint of a shrug. 'These things aren't proof – you know that as well as I do. But she passed.' He paused. 'I gotta wash up.'

The other two watched him go, then exchanged glances of quiet triumph. Although neither of them was going to admit it, they'd both taken quite a shine to Rikki Davis.

Chapter Seventeen

Brian Byrd adjusted his oiliest smile, while the fat diamond on his pinky-finger winked brightly across the Court. 'Okay, Laurie. Is it okay if I call you "Laurie"?'

'Yes.'

'That night in the bar,' Byrd said, 'you were dressed a little differently than you are right now, weren't you?'

'Yes.'

'Nice dress. Make-up. Would it be fair to say, you looked older?'

'I guess.'

'And the bartender served you alcohol?'

'We had fake I.D.s.'

'I see.' Byrd's oily features hardened. 'Did you ever tell Mr Baldwin that you were under the age of eighteen?'

'No.'

'And before he sat next to you, did any other men in the lounge try to – y'know, hit on you?'

'A couple' – she hesitated, drawing her forefinger along the rail of the witness stand.

Byrd nodded, 'You looked pretty adult that night, didn't you, Laurie?'

'Objection,' said Zoey.

'I'll withdraw it.' Byrd smiled again at Laurie. 'Why did you and your girlfriend go to a hotel lounge?'

'I already said. We were bored. And we were looking for something to do.'

'Uh-huh.' Byrd paused, studying for a moment the diamond on his finger; then raised his head and said, in a friendly, matter-of-fact tone, 'You carry condoms in your purse, don't you, Laurie?'

'*Objection*,' cried Zoey.

'Goes to consent, Your Honour,' Byrd said.

Judge McGrath nodded, 'All right.'

Byrd turned again to the girl on the stand. 'You carry condoms in your purse, don't you?' he repeated.

The girl said quickly, 'Yes – because my mother wants me to. To be safe if I ever . . .'

'You were out looking for sex that night,' Byrd said brutally.

'Objection,' Zoey said again; but before the Judge could rule, the girl shouted:

'No! And I never told *him* I wanted to have sex with him.'

'How many drinks had you consumed that night?' Byrd went on smoothly.

'Two.'

'Were you inebriated?'

'I don't know.'

'Maybe a little?'

'Maybe.'

'And when you started to kiss, it became, well – passionate, did it not?'

'I don't know.'

'Well – you said the kissing became heavy,' Byrd said, with an insinuating grin.

'That didn't mean he could do what he did,' she replied, sniffing.

'Did you put your hands on his buttocks?' There was no reply. 'Did you grab his buttocks and pull them into you?' Byrd persisted.

Laurie bit her lip, her hand quivering on the rail. 'I don't remember.'

'So it's possible you did?'

Zoey was on her feet. 'The witness said she doesn't remember,' she cried.

'Move on, Mr Byrd,' ordered Judge McGrath.

Byrd faced the girl and paused, 'What did you do immediately after the two of you made love?'

'We didn't make love. He raped me.'

'After it was over, what'd you do?'

'I left. I went to the lobby and got a cab.'

'Did you report to hotel security that you'd been raped?'

'No, I just got out of there.'

'And where'd you go?'

'Home.'

'Not to the hospital. Not to the police.'

'I just wanted to get home.' Her voice suddenly feeble, exhausted, broken.

Byrd pressed on, pitilessly. 'And when you *arrived* home, your mother was waiting for you, wasn't she, Laurie? And she was very upset. Dressed the way you were. All that make-up – two-thirty in the morning – and you come home drunk without your panties.'

'Objection!' cried Zoey.

'You were afraid of what she'd do so you *made up* the story of being raped, isn't that right, Laurie?'

'Objection' – Zoey was on her feet again, while the girl spluttered:

'That's not true! He raped me!'

'Come on, Laurie' – Byrd's smile was like the cat who's just seen the mouse served up with cream. 'You really would rather commit perjury than have your mother find out the truth?'

'*Objection!*'

'Withdrawn.' Byrd shrugged and gave Laurie a little fake smile of sympathy. 'Y'know . . . You seem like a very nice young lady. I hope you realise that these lies are hurting an innocent man.'

'Move to strike that,' Zoey cried.

'Sustained,' said Judge McGrath, frowning. 'C'mon, Mr Byrd.'

'I have nothing further,' said Byrd, and turned; this time his oily smile was directed deliberately at the Jury.

*

The first face up on the screen was a pleasant smiling mug-shot of a man in his seventies, in an open-necked shirt and Fair Isle sweater.

'This here's the deceased – Harold Davis,' Tommy Mullaney said, from behind the projector. 'Before . . .' – he removed the slide and snapped in another – 'and after . . .'

A low collective cry went up from the darkened room, '*Oh, look at that!*' – terrible! . . . Oh my God! . . . How horrible . . .!'

The static image that had now flashed up on the screen

158

showed the bulky, misshapen figure of a man in a business suit, the trouser-legs pulled up from the ankles and stretched tight round the groin, his shoes pointing downwards and his head twisted sideways, as his whole body hung from a noose that had squeezed his neck to the width of a child's wrist.

'Wait,' Mullaney drawled, with a hint of morbid delight. 'This next one's even better . . .'

The screen went dark, as he changed to the next slide; and this time the cries of disgust out of the darkness were even louder. On the screen there now appeared, in vivid enlarged close-up, the face of Harold Davis, barely recognisable – horribly swollen and bent to one side, the lips black, the eyes bulging and sightless.

'Unbelievable!' breathed Brackman, with childlike wonder, 'Look at his face! *Is he blue?*'

'He ain't happy,' Mullaney mused, with laconic brutality, as he flicked to the next picture. This showed a close-up of the dead man's head on the autopsy table: a dark smudged welt across the wrinkled skin of the neck, and a black mark on the top of his balding head.

'Victim also had a bruise, top of the forehead,' Mullaney intoned. 'They might be saying the killer knocked him out cold before stringing him up.'

Another click: and the screen showed the close-up of what looked like an elaborate mousetrap lying on the carpeted floor.

'The guy's teeth,' Mullaney said. 'The cord must've squeezed 'em right out of his head.'

Click – and a big, handsome, blond boy with a smile as wide as Wilshire Boulevard was leering out at them, as though to say, '*C'mon, baby, slip into something loose and let's go for a drive on the beach . . .*'

'Oooh,' cried Abby out of the darkness, 'What a *hunk . . .*'

'Now we're talking,' C.J. said.

'The boyfriend,' Mullaney explained. 'Name of David Shaeffer.'

'Guilty,' somebody said, and they all laughed.

'His trial is separate,' said Mullaney. 'Starts in about two weeks.'

'Abby, I want you to monitor that,' Kuzak said.

'Absolutely.'

Mullaney continued, from behind the projector, 'This guy, Shaeffer, and Rikki had been friendly about eight months. They broke up after the arrests. Murder can be brutal on a relationship,' he added laconically. He clicked to the next slide, showing a smart, good-looking blonde woman in her late thirties. 'The victim's daughter,' Mullaney explained. 'Cut out of the will. We gotta do some digging on her . . .'

The next slide put up a smiling eighty-year-old woman with a lot of white hair, like one of those cheerful old Norman Rockwell portraits of American homestead life.

'. . . Mildred Spicer. Next door neighbour. Would come over twice a week and scratch the victim's feet. Has a criminal record for kleptomania . . .'

Next up was a big, handsome white mansion behind a colonial-style porch and a lawn decorated with lush tropical shrubs. 'Victim's house,' Tommy drawled. 'Rich pigs . . .'

Kuzak called out of the darkness, 'Stuart, I want you to pore over the will. See if anybody besides Rikki stands to take.'

160

There was another click, and this time the screen was blank. 'That's all the photos in the police file,' Mullaney said, as the lights in the room came on.

Kuzak, in his chair at the end of the row, turned to the others, 'All right, look. If we're gonna win this thing we have to either hand the jury another suspect or sell suicide. We have to pick one thing and go with it. In the meantime, I'm calling a Press conference. The media's putting out stuff on this every day and since would-be jurors are probably reading it, I want to get our version in print too, as fast as possible. Abby, I need the motion to suppress by Friday. Jonathan, same thing for the change of venue. C.J., you work the private investigation team. Stuart, go to work on the will. Okay, that's all.'

They all stood up. Brackman smoothed down his suit, straightened his tie, and said, 'I want an acquittal here, people.'

Rollins muttered thoughtfully, as though to no-one in particular, 'That was a Gordian knot. He had to have help.'

'The boyfriend did it,' Markowitz said confidently.

'Nope,' said Abby. 'Too cute.'

C.J. nodded. 'Way too cute,' she murmured.

Chapter Eighteen

Judge McGrath surveyed the crowded Criminal Court-room and nodded: 'All right. Let's bring her in.'

An usher moved forward and the doors opened at the side of the Court. Laurie Penn came in, slowly, led by a Court official. At first few people in the Courtroom recognised her. Her hair was up, her faced masked in make-up; her plump youthful body encased in a clinging black miniskirt and pink, patent-leather high-heeled shoes, like a pair of tiny stilts. She paused just inside the doorway, her head bowed – conscious that the eyes of the whole Court were upon her.

'Members of the Jury,' Judge McGrath said, severely, without discernible pity. 'The parties stipulate that Ms Penn's appearance today fairly reflects the way she appeared on the night in question.' He paused, looking directly at the girl in the doorway, 'Ms Penn. Please walk up and stand before the Jury.'

Slowly, led by the Court official, Laurie Penn began to hobble forward, her head still bowed, and stopped, visibly humiliated, in front of the jury-box.

Byrd was on his feet, flashing his ringed finger in front of him. 'Your Honour, I'd like for her to turn to the side.'

The Judge nodded, looking at the girl, 'Ms Penn?'

She turned slowly, like an awkward mannequin on the catwalk.

'Okay,' Byrd said. 'Now please turn around – put your back to the Jury.'

She turned, again, almost tripping on her high-heels, and displayed her neat little rump to the two rows of embarrassed Jury members. Her face, behind the lavish make-up, was stiff with the effort of preventing herself from bursting into tears. Her humiliation was now total, agonising.

'Okay, that's enough,' the Judge ordered. 'You can sit down now, Ms Penn. Mr Byrd, make your closing statement.'

Byrd smiled widely round the Court, pausing on the Jury. 'Well,' he said, in his rich unctuous voice, 'I think young Laurie Penn just made it for me. How could any red-blooded American male not be attracted to that?'

He paused, with an eloquent, knowing shrug. 'The bartender believed her to be twenty-one. Several patrons did. My client did. And you can certainly see why. What a beautiful woman she is!' He stood leering at her for a moment, then looked straight past her at the Jury:

'As for consent? Ladies and gentlemen . . . she dressed herself up like that – equipped herself with condoms – camped out at a hotel bar. She *willingly* went to my client's suite, willingly *kissed* him, fondled him, eventually made love to him. Then, faced with a touch of guilt and a disapproving mother, she made up a story. And she got caught up in that story, when mom went to the police. And now Orin Baldwin is entangled in it too.'

163

He paused again, striding purposefully forward until he was close to the jury-box, standing almost directly in front of the terrified girl. 'I won't assault your dignity,' he went on, 'by wasting a lot of time trying to convince you there's reasonable doubt here. You already must know that. Was Orin Baldwin guilty of bad judgement that night? Perhaps. But rape?' – and he spread his hands contemptuously – 'Well, that's just ridiculous.' His eyes swivelled onto the trembling girl who stood only a few inches away from him, '*Ridiculous*,' he added, with ruthless disdain; then, after a deep breath, he gave the Jury a last confiding smile, and returned triumphantly to his seat.

Zoey Clemmons slowly rose, faced the Jury, and, with a quick reassuring smile to Laurie Penn, began her closing argument:

'She dressed the way sixteen-year-olds dress these days. They grow up watching Madonna videos – the black lingerie' – she gave a sad, resigned shrug – 'sexy is in. It's hip. And the condoms in her purse . . .? We *teach* our children to carry condoms! And with the AIDS epidemic, don't you dare accept his suggestion that to do so is evidence of consent. And yes – she kissed him – maybe she even grabbed his buttocks. But she also did something else. She said 'no'. Laurie Penn pushed the defendant away and told him '*No*.' She turned suddenly and glared down at the hunched figure of Orin Baldwin, whose coarse face was flushed, dark and sweaty.

'And *he*,' she went on, 'responded with violent forced intercourse. That's rape. It isn't sex. It isn't making love. It's rape. And she's here today, willing to be judged by you – willing to relive that vicious attack . . . because that's the only way to make the point – the point that *every* woman,

whether sixteen or sixty – still has the right to say "stop".
You don't forfeit it when you kiss a man. Even lying on a
bed . . . there is *never* a point, ladies and gentlemen, where
if she says "no," the man is *entitled* to overpower her. That's
why she's here. *To make that one simple point.* A point that
Orin Baldwin refused to get that night.' She turned, glaring
again at the defendant, 'Please see that he gets it today.'

She stopped and returned, almost breathless, to her seat.

*

It was stifling in the Criminal Court as a dead silence fell
and the Jury filed slowly in and took their places. Little
Laurie Penn, dressed in plain grey skirt and white blouse,
sat crouched between her ashen-faced mother and Zoey
Clemmons, who waited with well-trained, inscrutable
patience.

'Mr Foreman,' Judged McGrath called down: 'The Jury
has returned with a verdict?'

The Foreman at the end of the row nodded gravely, 'Yes,
Your Honour. On the count of 3274, Statutory Rape, we
find the defendant, Orin Baldwin – *not guilty*.'

There was a slight stir across the Court, and Zoey
Clemmons lowered her head. But the Foreman of the Jury
was not finished. 'On the count 3275, Rape, we find the
defendant, Orin Baldwin . . . *guilty as charged*.'

A great roar of approval burst across the packed
Courtroom. Zoey Clemmons leapt to her feet and, disregarding all conventions, all appearance of being neutral,
pulled Laurie Penn to her feet and kissed her on both
cheeks, then turned and hugged the mother, who was
already weeping with relief.

While the Judge was already dismissing the Jury, Zoey was swallowing back her tears. 'Oh God,' she said, hugging Laurie again, 'the rule is we should never celebrate in the Courtroom. But I don't care . . .!'

'Ms Clemmons . . .!' Judge McGrath called down.

Zoey straightened up, collecting herself in a hurry, 'Oh – I'm sorry, Your Honour. The people ask that bail be revoked and the defendant be taken into custody.'

'Opposed,' Byrd snarled, from the defendant's table, where Orin Baldwin sat slumped forward, his face the colour of cold porridge.

Judge McGrath nodded, 'It is so ordered. The Court officers will take him into custody.'

'Your Honour,' Byrd began again; but the Judge cut him short. 'Forget it, Counsel.'

Already Shirley Penn was leading her daughter down the aisle. Zoey Clemmons watched them sadly, wondering what would happen to the child – whether this marked a happy watershed in her life, or just the first of many grim jolts on a downward path.

Through another door, at the side of the Court, the big lumbering figure of Orin Baldwin was being escorted by two officials towards a bleak and brutal future. Behind him padded Byrd, anticipating his fee, like an obedient dog sniffing its dinner . . .

*

Tommy Mullaney stood stiffly to attention, with Mike Kuzak at his side.

'Ladies and gentlemen of the Jury,' he began, 'my name is Tommy Mullaney. My partner is Michael Kuzak and, together, we represent the woman sitting right there. Her name is Rikki Davis. 'Now –' his voice faltered for a moment – 'I'm sure you've read a lot about this lady . . . but – *oh shoot* . . .!' He gagged, wheeled round from the washroom mirror and ducked his head over the toilet.

Mike Kuzak waited for the sounds of retching to subside. 'Maybe you got the flu,' he said at last.

Mullaney, still crouched on all fours, shook his head miserably. 'It ain't flu,' he groaned, his voice booming back at them out of the lavatory bowl. 'It's goddam nerves! These big trials make me nauseous.'

Kuzak hesitated. He didn't want to sound unfeeling towards his friend, but this was hardly the moment to go into a swoon. 'Maybe *I* should open?' he began, just as Mullaney vomited again.

'No. No, Mike – I'm okay,' Tommy staggered to his feet, the sweat standing out on his brow. 'Feelin' better by the second!' he added, with a fearful grin. 'This is a good thing, Mike – it means I'm ready . . .'

'You look awful,' Kuzak said.

Mullaney moved slowly towards the basins, sank his head down and splashed water over his face and hair and neck; then straightened up, with a deep sigh, saying, 'Glen Hall – best goalie in the history of hockey – used to puke before every game.' He grinned again, brighter this time. 'Means ya' ready, that's all.' He slapped his side. 'I'm pumped,' he added, starting towards the door.

Kuzak followed, frowning slightly. 'Good. We leave here in ten minutes. And I forgot to tell you – the Judge said "yes" to cameras in the Courtroom.'

'Great,' Mullaney said, quickening his step out of the door.

'You coming to the staff meeting?' Kuzak called after him, as they entered the office complex.

'Yeah, in just a second. I wanna go over it a coupla times first.'

Kuzak caught up with him and grinned. 'We're gonna kick ass on this one, Tommy!'

Mullaney turned. 'You know it, huh?' But the words died on his lips. His face had turned green again, as he lurched back through the door and headed once more for the restroom.

*

Douglas Brackman banged the Conference Room table, calling for silence, 'Okay, people – settle in! First up' – he nodded to McKenzie, on his left – 'Happy birthday, Leland McKenzie.' He paused, po-faced. 'How old are you, Leland?'

'A hundred and two,' McKenzie growled. 'Move along.'

'Okay – first item on the agenda. The big day is finally upon us – the People versus Rikki Davis.' He glanced down the table, 'Michael . . .?'

'We open in an hour,' Kuzak said, nodding. 'We're ready.' Nobody seemed to have noticed Mullaney's absence.

'Excellent. We'll have a Command Post set up here in the Conference Room. Any surprises come up at the trial, we'll have lawyers here ready to jump.'

'We gonna win?' Becker asked, half-sceptically; then looked up, as the door opened and Mullaney came in.

'We could,' Kuzak replied aggressively. 'I like our Jury draw – and I like Judge Gates.'

Mullaney crept quietly to a chair at the end of the table.

'Cook's one of the best D.A.s in town,' Kuzak continued, 'but his case has holes.'

Grace Van Owen spoke up beside him, 'Just keep him offguard wherever you can, Mike. Disrupt his rhythm – he doesn't like that – makes him less effective.'

'We'll be on to him – every chance we get,' Kuzak assured her.

Tommy's voice came from the end of the table, 'We held back a coupla motions – just so we could spring the objections at the trial. Put him back on his heels a little.' He sounded confident, almost jaunty.

'Good idea,' Grace said.

Brackman cut in, 'Every lawyer here stands to assist. With all the publicity, we want that acquittal.'

'You'll get it,' Kuzak said, nodding down at Mullaney, 'won't he, Tommy?'

'Sure will,' Mullaney said, with a tired wolf's grin.

Chapter Nineteen

The street outside the L.A. Courthouse was lined with high-sided television vans; on the steps leading up to the entrance, little knots of people crowded round instant TV interviews with VIPs and local dignitaries connected with the case. Inside the building, the halls and corridors were jammed with a seething, surging mob of reporters, attorneys, High-Society groupies, sundry celebrities and the usual murder aficionados who gravitated to these big trials like wasps to a jam pot.

Somehow, as though by a magician's sleight of hand, with deft organisation and footwork on the part of the local police and Court security men, Rikki Davis and her entourage – which included Kuzak and Mullaney, one at each elbow – were spirited into the main Criminal Court.

Cameras clicked all round them like crickets; flash-guns exploded in their faces, half-blinding them before they got into the Courtroom. Rikki Davis was protected by wrap-around dark glasses that concealed most of her lovely face under a wide-brimmed black hat.

A gang of TV reporters closed in, yelling at the procession as it reached the doors of the Court:

'. . . *Mr Kuzak, will Rikki be testifying . . .?*'

'*Is it true you rejected a last-minute plea bargain . . .?*'

A young woman reporter with a large red mouth was shouting at a handcam, '. . . *Wearing a sleek black designer suit – skirt above the knee – she looks very elegant indeed . . .*'

'. . . *How significant is the venue for this trial, Mr Mullaney . . .?*'

Kuzak and Mullaney, with their beautiful client pressed between them, answered none of these questions as they were swept relentlessly, by the tide of the crowd, through the double doors into the packed Courtroom.

*

Inside, the atmosphere was somewhere between a First Night audience on Broadway and the prelude to a highly charged political meeting. Some of the Press reports, inevitably, described it as the 'Rikki Davis Circus'.

It took a phalanx of security men to part the crowds, beat back the reporters and cameras, and make a path for Rikki Davis's party to reach the front of the Court.

Judge Gary Gates, a small grey man with a sharp wit and a pair of eyebrows like miniature gorse bushes, looked down from the bench with animated disapproval. But if this was how City Hall wanted to play it – and some of the boys up there, he thought, ought to have Press agents, the way they revelled in the publicity – then, as a humble Law officer, he wasn't gonna rule it out of order. (The security alone, he thought, must be costing L.A.'s taxpayers a few million – but then, it was good show business . . . .)

As they took their seats at the defendant's table, Kuzak and Mullaney acknowledged the quick, formal nod of their opposite number for the Prosecution – Assistant District Attorney Newell Cook, a handsome dark man in his late forties, with a deep suntan and the physique of an athlete. Kuzak and Mullaney often played tennis with him at the Athletic Club: they knew he had a hard backhand, and a bad temper when he dropped a serve.

Kuzak nodded to his partner. 'All set?'

'All set,' Mullaney said, and belched. He put a hand to his lips. 'Excuse me.'

Rikki Davis sat erect between them, impassive. Her expression, behind the wrap-around glasses, was invisible; any pallor in her cheeks lightly dusted away with make-up.

Judge Gates banged his gavel several times for silence. 'Counsel – approach, please,' he called down.

Kuzak, Mullaney and Newell Cook rose and stepped forward. The air all round was full of the frenzied clicking of cameras. Judge Gates leaned forward and growled down at the three of them. 'Despite my warning at the pre-trial, you've all continued to showboat with the Press.' His voice was heavy with admonition.

Kuzak shrugged, nodding at his tennis partner, Newell Cook. '*He's* the one who's been making statements, Your Honour. We've just been responding.'

'I don't care,' snapped the Judge. 'The reason I let the cameras in here was to remove the need for any of you to distort the events. So let's just try the case, gentlemen. No grandstand plays – no stunts.' He paused, 'Are we listening, Mr Mullaney?'

'It's just another trial to me, Judge,' Tommy Mullaney drawled laconically. Kuzak looked at him warily: but he looked as relaxed now as a bouncer at a High School prom.

'Okay,' Judge Gates said dubiously. 'Let's go.'

'It was the perfect crime,' Newell Cook told the Court, his voice cutting cleanly through the tense, crowded stillness. 'The victim was despondent over cancer – so he just strung himself up. The grieving shocked widow discovers the body, calls the police, everybody cries, the will gets probated and Rikki Davis inherits twenty-six million dollars.' He paused, long enough to allow the significance of this to have its full, damaging effect.

'I'm sure the original plan,' he continued, with a trace of deadly irony, 'when she married this old man with cancer was just to wait patiently for his death. She had her lover on the side – it wasn't as if she were making such a sacrifice. But when Harold Davis suddenly decided to divorce her, the game-plan was ruined. She'd lose everything by virtue of a prenuptial agreement. And she wasn't going to let that happen. Oh no! So she and her lover, David Shaeffer – motivated solely by greed – staged an apparent suicide.' He paused, with an actor's perfect timing:

'They hanged Harold Davis. They hanged him until he was dead.'

The silence broke for a moment: there was a rippling murmur across the Court, and the cameras were clicking again. Cook continued, 'That's what the evidence will show, ladies and gentlemen. Rikki Davis murdered her husband for his money. Clean and simple, that's what the evidence will show.' He turned and went back to his seat.

There was a very slight pause; then Mullaney rose to his feet. 'Ladies and gentlemen of the Jury. My name is Tommy Mullaney –' his voice was a little hoarse, perhaps even slower than usual, but otherwise fully under control – 'my

173

partner is Michael Kuzak, and together we represent that woman sitting right there. Her name is Rikki Davis. Now I'm sure you've read a lot about this lady and – if you've been reading the same papers as me – you *gotta* be thinking she's guilty. I know *I* thought that the day she walked into our office for the first time. But then we started piecin' together the facts. Then, when she passed our lie-detector test, we thought —'

'Mr Mullaney, that's out of line,' Judge Gates broke in, anticipating Newell Cook, who was on his feet, crying, '*Objection!*'

'You know better than that!' the Judge added, glaring furiously down at Mullaney.

Mullaney nodded. 'Sorry.'

Kuzak gulped back a smile and glanced surreptitiously at Rikki Davis, who appeared not to notice him.

Judge Gates growled, 'The Jury will disregard that remark. Polygraph tests are *not* deemed reliable – you're to give that statement no weight whatsoever.' He turned again, glowering at the defendant's table: 'Don't test me, Mr Mullaney.'

Tommy bowed his head, in righteous, almost theatrical, contrition. 'I apologise. You see . . . ladies and gentlemen. That's what the evidence will show . . .' But the damage was done: the Jury now knew about the lie-detector, and no amount of wrath from Judge Gates could wipe their memory of it.

Mullaney struggled to get back on track. 'Hanging's a very tricky thing,' he told the Court. 'Easy for it to go wrong. Rikki had access to his medication. She coulda drugged him to death. She knew where he kept his gun. She had easier ways to stage a suicide if that's what she wanted to do. But hanging him? That's tough. Why would she choose that way to do it?'

He paused, took a drink of water from the table. Kuzak glanced uneasily at him: his voice was still calm, but there was a faint film of sweat on his upper lip.

'And why would she discover the body with her lover?' he went on. 'And so draw attention to her infidelity? Does that make sense to you? No – it's too easy. But that's where they're fingering her, ladies and gentlemen. They're doing it *because* it's easy.' He gave a half-smile:

'My ex-wife's an A.D.A. – she'd tell me they *gotta* pick the easy targets sometimes' – he shrugged. 'The Department's undermanned – they don't have time to flush out the facts —'

'What is this!' Newell Cook cried, springing to his feet.

'Mr Mullaney,' Judge Gates said, 'just stick to this case.'

Mullaney rounded on Cook, 'I know you gotta be feelin' conflicted here . . .'

'Mr Mullaney,' Gates said furiously, 'knock it off, will you' – and, against a swelling roar from across the Courtroom, he vented his full fury on Mullaney. 'You will *not* address the Assistant District Attorney! You will *not* comment on him or burden this Court with any of your opinions. Just stick to the case.'

Mullaney was sweating badly now. 'The thing is,' he began again, turning to the Jury, 'there *is* no case. We got a dead guy – no question about that. We got a defendant with a motive – no argument there either. *But there isn't any case.*' He began speaking more rapidly now, moving towards the Jury and addressing them directly, face-to-face:

'You pay attention here! We're gonna pull the curtain off the Prosecution's dog-and-pony show. You listen to their witnesses – listen to *everything* – and you'll be acquitting Rikki Davis. This, I know.' He stood in front of them, nodding vigorously. 'My only request here,' he added, taking a deep breath, 'is that *you all pay attention*. If you *do*, we won't have to ask you for anything else. I promise . . .'

He broke off and started back to his chair. Kuzak could now see the sweat spreading across Mullaney's taut face, gleaming in the television lights.

*

Leland McKenzie stared dotingly across the little table, blushing like a schoolboy.

'You . . . you didn't . . .' he stammered, 'you didn't have to get me anything . . .'

Rosalind Shays gave him her softest enamelled smile, lowering her blonde eyelashes. 'Well, at your age, birthdays are at a premium. Supply and demand, you know?' she added, with a coy smile.

There were back in Tribeca's Restaurant, in their usual velvet alcove; and had just finished their *marrons glacés*, helped down with a fashionable Californian dry white. They were both happy, buoyed up with an almost adolescent sentimentality for each other's company.

'Go on – aren't you going to open it?'

'Very touching,' he murmured, inadequately; he began tearing awkwardly at the flimsy mauve wrapping-paper in front of him; and finally drew out a slim black box, opening it to reveal a flat square platinum watch. He lifted his head and their eyes met.

'Oh my . . . this is beautiful, Rosalind!'

'You like it?' she said, beaming nervously back at him.

176

'It's fantastic. But it's too much. It's way, *way* too much!'

'There's an inscription on the back,' she said softly – all the power-dressed aggression of the modern L.A. woman gone now: she was like an excited schoolgirl at her first prom.

Leland McKenzie had turned the little watch over and began carefully reading, through his bifocals, '*Just say yes*'. He looked up and said stupidly, 'Yes to what?'

Rosalind Shays leaned across the table and folded one hand across his. 'Leland, will you marry me?'

For a moment McKenzie seemed not to have heard correctly. 'C'mon – yes to what?'

Her hand closed firmly over his. 'I'm serious, Leland. I don't mean to shock you. I'm usually the master of subtlety, but I don't know how to tiptoe into something like this. I've been so happy the last four months . . .' She shrugged nervously. 'Well, I'm not a young gal any more – and I know what I want.'

McKenzie was sitting forward, his lips parted, his eyes stricken. He swallowed a couple of times and said, 'You want . . . *me*?'

'I do. I want to be your wife.'

*

'Detective Foley's up first.' Tommy was leaning against the wall of Kuzak's office, looking directly down at Rikki Davis in the client's chair. He was trying hard to keep it impersonal – trying not to notice the lovely lines of her body inside the plain, linen, perfectly tailored white suit. 'He's the key,' he added. 'We gotta do some damage to him.'

Across the table Mike Kuzak listened impassively.

'What's his testimony?' Rikki asked.

'All the physical evidence,' Mullaney said. 'They got your husband's lawyer to get in motive. But all the evidence of foul play' – he shrugged loosely – 'well, that comes with this guy.'

'If I can trip him up,' said Kuzak, 'we're off to the races.'

'What about me?' said Rikki. 'When do I testify?'

Kuzak and Mullhaney looked at each other for a long moment. Kuzak was frowning. 'I don't know that I'm putting you up there,' he told her at last.

'Why not?'

'The truth is' – Kuzak wasn't looking at her as he spoke – 'you come off unlikeable, Rikki. I don't like to say it, but the Jury are going to read you as cold.' He watched her stiffen in her chair, but she stayed silent.

'I also think Cook will dissect you on the adultery,' he went on, 'and nobody'll care two cents about you after he's done.'

Rikki Davis looked vaguely worried: but angry too. 'But if I don't take the stand – it'll look like I'm hiding something.'

'Maybe,' he said, 'but still . . .'

'Better to *hide* what I am,' she said excitedly, 'than let them actually see it . . .?' Neither of them answered her. She went on, the emotion rising in her voice – the first true indicator of her personality they'd yet seen. 'Now, you listen to me – both of you!' she cried. 'I don't want to be buried away in this – shielded from the Jury because I'm the selfish bitch in this case, just like the Press keep calling me!' She was half out of her chair now, rounding on them both in turn:

'I'm not that person, *damn it*! and I don't want to be

178

treated like that person. Not by them – not by *you* – not by anybody! You understand me?'

Kuzak's face was blank and hard. 'You want the whole world to think better of you, Rikki?' – he let his hand drop flatly on the desk – 'Then hire a publicity agent. You want to escape a murder conviction, you do what your lawyers tell you.' He leaned forward and looked her firmly in the eye. 'Right now, we say you don't testify.'

Her lovely mouth went slack at the corners. 'Who the hell do you think you are, talking to me —' Her voice was almost a snarl, but Kuzak cut it short:

'This is a murder trial, Ms Davis. Tomorrow morning, I've gotta face off against a seasoned Homicide Detective. And I tell you – this guy Foley's a pro.' He nodded grimly, 'I have a lotta work here. So get your ego out of our faces, and let us do what we do.'

Her mask of calm detachment had collapsed; and for a moment she looked about to crumple into tears. She lowered her head, sniffed a couple of times, and muttered, 'I'm sorry.'

Tommy shifted against the wall and said gently, 'We know you're scared, Rikki. Everybody's a little scared. But you gotta trust us.' He gave her a little lopsided smile. 'You just got to.'

*

Ann Kelsey hadn't been in Leland McKenzie's office more than five minutes, when she knew she wasn't getting his full attention. They were ploughing through the final proofs of the firm's prospectus – a task requiring absolute attention to detail, especially from the Senior Partner.

She was sitting next to him at his desk, tapping the glossy proofs with her silver pencil. 'I still think we have a problem with the profit definition,' she told him. 'It's ambiguous at best, and that'll be construed against *us* if anything goes wrong . . .'

She glanced sideways and saw Leland staring blankly at the empty beige wall opposite the office window. 'Leland,' she began, 'are you listening to me?'

He caught himself in time, smiled, and said hurriedly, 'Yes . . . Yes . . . Go on.'

'Leland – what's the matter?' She tapped the proofs with her hand. 'This stuff is tough enough without you drifting off into outer space.'

'I'm sorry –' He tried to smile, but it turned into a frown. 'Ann, I . . . Last night – well –' He seemed about to chew his lower lip but pressed on. 'Last night Rosalind Shays proposed to me.'

It was Ann Kelsey's turn to frown. 'Proposed what?' she asked.

McKenzie gulped. 'Marriage. She gave me a beautiful Cartier watch and asked me . . .' – he gulped again – 'to be her husband.'

For a moment she struggled valiantly to conceal her horror. 'How exciting,' she murmured, with a stillborn smile.

'Do you think . . .?' McKenzie began to fidget frantically with a stainless steel pen set on the desk; then suddenly met Ann's eyes. 'Well, what do you think about the two of us? As a couple, I mean . . .?'

'You seem very . . . cute?' she replied enigmatically.

'Could you see yourself standing at our wedding ceremony?' he asked.

180

She swallowed hard, trying to give herself time to think. 'I'm sure it would be lovely, Leland.'

'The truth, Ann,' he demanded.

She looked him in the eye again and said, 'I'd sooner dive head-first into a basinful of my own vomit.'

'Ann!' McKenzie was perhaps more shocked by the imagery of her words than by their content.

'Dating her is one thing, Leland' – (She was in so deep now, she might as well go the whole hog, and to hell with Leland's finer feelings!) – 'sleeping with her is another,' she went on. 'But exchanging wedding vows with a person who can shed her own skin and swallow large rats whole is something –'

'I don't need *that much* truth,' he snapped, beginning to redden.

But Ann, once started, wasn't going to let him off the hook so easily. 'Leland, how could you *possibly* think of marrying that woman? You have nothing in common – you know nothing about . . .'

McKenzie broke in. 'I'm lonely, Ann.' He paused, then began nodding slowly. 'Rosalind and I . . . we laugh together – we have a wonderful, intellectual relationship. I'm sixty-two years old, Ann, and loneliness is everything they say it is.'

She felt desperately sorry for him: wanted to help him, reassure him, give him the most positive advice she could, which meant – which had to mean – telling it like it really was. The hard, brutal, unvarnished truth. 'Do you love her?' she said at last.

'I'm very fond of her,' McKenzie said.

'You're fond of her,' she repeated. 'I'm sorry, Leland, I'm certainly no marriage guidance expert. My first one ended

181

in divorce – and Stuart and I . . .' She gave an enigmatic shrug. 'Well, we have our problems, too. But at the core of it all, I love him – and I trust him more than anyone else I've ever known . . . or ever *will* know.' She paused, catching her breath. Leland made no response.

'Can you say that about Rosalind?' she asked, mercilessly.

Leland avoided her eyes. He spoke quickly. 'I'm not asking myself those kinds of questions. It's a much simpler test. I know my life without her. I've seen my life *with* her. I'm happier *with* her. That's all there is to it.'

Chapter Twenty

Detective John Foley was a sandy-haired man in his forties, with pale eyes and a pinched white nose which gave him a hard, oddly ascetic look. He stood erect, in uniform, answering the Prosecution's questions from the stand.

To the side, in full view of the jury-box, a large blown-up photograph of the late Harold Davis' head had been mounted on an easel – the rope burns and livid scratch marks on the neck, and the bruise on the top of the head, all clearly visible; but, for the benefit of any sceptics, the injuries had been highlighted with red crayon on a plastic overlay.

'Detective Foley,' Newell Cook said, 'did the Coroner's report state the cause of death?'

'Asphyxiation by strangulation. The victim was hanged.'

'Objection,' said Mullaney. 'We all know the guy was hung.'

Cook scowled, 'Your Honour, I object to this harassment.'

Judge Gates frowned down at Mullaney. 'Counsel.'

'I apologise,' said Tommy, and resumed his seat.

Newell Cook continued. 'Detective – when you arrived at the scene – what did the defendant tell you?'

'That she and Mr Shaeffer had returned to the house to find the deceased' – he gave a quick glance across at Mullaney –'*suspended* from the ceiling. She stated that it was her belief that Mr Davis had taken his own life.'

'Did the evidence support her belief?'

'No, it did not.'

'Why not, Detective?'

'Well, first off, you can see the scrape marks around the neck, indicating that the victim tried to free himself. Second, we dusted the cord and the beam and found one clean print belonging to the defendant. We also found a partial print which matched David Shaeffer.'

'They said these prints got there when they attempted to cut the victim down, after discovering him.'

'If that were true,' Foley said, 'their prints would've been all over the beam and cord. The fact that we found just the one suggests somebody tried to wipe the surface clean and just wasn't careful enough.'

'What other evidence pointed you to the defendant?'

'The will,' said Foley. 'That established a substantial monetary motive. The defendant also had no alibi, except to say she went for a drive with Mr Shaeffer following their brunch together.'

'Did you confront her with your suspicions?' Cook asked.

'Yes, she said she wanted to talk to her lawyer.'

Cook nodded. 'Thank you, Detective. Nothing further.'

He took his seat, and Kuzak stood up.

'Any sign of a struggle in the bedroom, Detective?'

'No, sir.'

'Isn't that strange? I mean, do you think they put the cord round his neck and politely asked him to stand on the chair while they tied the other end to the beam?'

'We believe he was rendered unconscious first,' Foley answered tonelessly.

'Oh, that's right' – Kuzak nodded, consulting a document in front of him. 'Yes, according to your initial report . . . you believe the victim was struck on the forehead with a blunt object which knocked him unconscious – after which he was hanged.' He held up the document, 'This is your document – correct?'

'Yes.'

'So is this what happened?' Kuzak asked.

'No.'

'*No?*' Kuzak repeated: and sensed Newell Cook shifting uneasily in his seat at the Prosecutor's table.

'The autopsy revealed that he sustained that bruise after he was dead,' Foley said flatly. 'So he probably got hit on the head when the Investigation Team cut him down.'

Kuzak gave a slow nod, holding the Detective's eye, 'So you were wrong?'

Foley said, 'We now believe the victim was suffocated into a state of unconsciousness.'

'Really? And why do you believe that, Detective?'

'Well, the symptoms of suffocation would be identical to the hanging. So there'd be no evidence of it.'

'In other words,' Kuzak said, 'there *is* no evidence of it.' He waited for the answer, but there was none. 'Detective – if, in fact, the deceased had been suffocated into unconsciousness before he was hung, how do you explain these scratch marks' – he nodded towards the blown-up photograph on the easel – 'he supposedly got while trying to free himself?'

'He likely regained consciousness right before the hanging.'

'Any evidence of *that*?' said Kuzak.

Foley began to redden, all except his thin white nose whose pallor emphasised his sudden annoyance: 'Yes – the scratch marks. They definitely show this thing wasn't something he wanted to do.'

'Well, maybe he changed his mind,' Kuzak suggested amiably. 'Hanging is a brutal, horrible way to go, isn't it?'

Foley nodded, 'Yes.'

'Yeah,' Kuzak said, nodding too. 'In fact, you yourself investigated another suicide by hanging, three years ago, where the victim tried to claw himself free. Didn't you, Detective?'

'There was one such occasion – yes.'

Kuzak smiled. 'Yes. Thank you. Now, on the finger-prints. Weren't there many smudged unusable prints all over the cord and beam?'

'Yes.'

'And, Detective, isn't it possible that in their panic – in their frantic attempts to free Mr Davis from the noose – they smudged a lot of their own prints and only left a few clean ones?'

Foley's knuckles had stiffened on the rail in front of him. 'There was only *one* clean print,' he said tightly. 'The likelihood —'

But Kuzak cut him short: 'Could two people do what they said they did and only leave one clean print?'

'Well, it's not impossible, but . . .'

'Thank you, Detective. In fact,' Kuzak went on, hammering home his point, 'from all the *physical* evidence – Harold Davis *could've* committed suicide – right?'

Foley was red again, fumbling his words. 'Yeah, well, when I've taken into consideration the will – as well as the statements made —'

'I'll ask you again, Detective,' Kuzak broke in, 'and I'd appreciate your answering the question this time. From all the *physical* evidence, it's possible that he committed suicide. Yes or no?'

There was a hard silence. 'Yes,' Foley said finally. 'But I don't think he did.'

*

'Your Honour,' said Newell Cook. 'People call Marion Davis to the stand.'

An elegant, beautifully-dressed woman in her late thirties, with the poised confident air of one who knows she can still cause a whole roomful of heads to turn, had began to cross the Court, when Michael Kuzak jumped to his feet.

'The Defence objects to this witness being called, Your Honour.'

Wearily, Judge Gates motioned all three Counsel forward.

'No relevance,' Kuzak added, when he reached the bench.

Cook said, 'She's the victim's daughter, Judge. Mr Davis made certain statements to her regarding the defendant —'

'Hearsay,' Mullaney drawled. 'Inadmissible.'

'Dead man statute applies,' Cook said.

Mullaney rounded on him: 'What! – are you nuts?'

187

'It doesn't apply,' Kuzak added quickly.

'Quiet,' said Gates. 'We're not talking about this here.' He stood up, nodding briskly towards the little side-door behind; and the three of them filed out after him.

The corridor outside was quiet, empty, closed off by the security men. Judge Gates closed the door behind him and turned. 'Offer of proof?. . .' he demanded.

Newell Cook said, 'The victim told her that the defendant had been acting strage – that she seemed 'up' to something. This was the week before the murder.'

'That's prejudicial hearsay,' Mullaney cut in. 'The daughter hates Rikki Davis – and the father knew this. He coulda been sayin' this crap to appease her – we got no means of assuring reliability here.'

Judge Gates listened to this, frowning for a moment. 'He's right,' he said at last. 'I'm not putting her up there to stay that stuff.'

'Oh, c'mon!' Cook protested.

'It would be an irreversible error,' Gates went on. 'Who's the next witness?'

Newell Cook scowled, 'Mark Chelios – he's the victim's lawyer.'

'Objection,' said Mullaney, as Kuzak chimed in:

'We object to this witness, too, Your Honour. Hearsay again.'

'Plus attorney–client,' Mullaney added.

Newell Cook faced the Judge, his voice low, urgent, almost pleading. 'Your Honour – I *need* this witness. I need him to establish motive. He's the only person who can testify as to the victim's intent to divorce the defendant.' He nodded at Kuzak and Mullaney. 'That's why they want to shut him down.'

Tommy snarled quietly, 'It's still black-letter hearsay.'

'I'm going to allow it,' Judge Gates said at last.

Kuzak and Mullaney began to protest again but Gates cut them short, 'Yes, I am. That's final.'

Kuzak took a deep breath. 'Then I want to see Mr Chelios' files for discovery.'

'Privilege,' Cook said.

'No, no, no!' – Judge Gates was getting impatient now – 'You can't have it both ways, Mr Cook. You want the lawyer to testify – fine. But first you give all the files to the Defence. By three o'clock today. Not three-thirty. Not three-fifteen. *Three o'clock*. Witness'll take the stand tomorrow.'

He swung round and opened the door, back into the Courtroom.

*

The man who had taken the stand was plump and chubby-cheeked, with glossy black hair and the smooth, easy manner of the professional who makes a good living out of attending the rich. He had the kind of face that can turn from a polite simper to white-lipped fury without moving a muscle.

'You had been Mr Harold Davis' lawyer for how long, Mr Chelios?' Newell Cook asked him.

'Since 1978.'

'And under the terms of his most recent will, how much money did the defendant, Rikki Davis, stand to inherit?'

'As the lone beneficiary,' Chelios said, 'she stood to inherit the entire estate – valued at about twenty-six million dollars.'

189

'And, sir, if they were divorced?'

'The prenuptial agreement limited her to five hundred thousand.'

'And, Mr Chelios – when was the last time you spoke with the deceased, Harold Davis?'

'Five days before his death.'

'Could you tell us what was said?'

'Objection!' said Kuzak.

'Overruled,' said Judge Gates.

Kuzak resumed his seat, furious, while beside him Mullaney was frowning. Rikki Davis didn't move.

Newell Cook turned again to the witness. 'What did Mr Davis tell you, Mr Chelios?'

'He told me that he wanted to file for divorce from his wife, Rikki. She was being unfaithful to him and he wanted to terminate the marital relationship.'

'And five days later he was found hanged to death?'

'Yes.'

'Sir – who, other than the defendant, stood to gain from the defendant's death?'

'Nobody,' Chelios said. 'At least no individuals. If she survives she takes all. If she doesn't, it goes to the American Cancer Society.'

'And, sir – do you have any reason to believe Harold Davis was suicidal?'

'*Objection!*' Kuzak and Mullaney cried in unison.

'Overruled.' Judge Gates nodded at the stand. 'Answer the question.'

'He was *not* suicidal,' Chelios said firmly. 'He was up-beat and —'

Mullaney and Kuzak were both on their feet. 'You gotta be kidding!' Mullaney called out.

'No foundation to give expert testimony —' Kuzak began, but the Judge boomed back at him:

'Overruled.'

Kuzak was beside himself with rage. 'There was no disclosure as to this kind of testimony . . .' he started.

'Sit down, Mr Kuzak,' Judge Gates ordered, 'or I'll hold you in contempt.'

Newell Cook had watched this intervention with evident satisfaction. He turned again to the stand. 'Continue, Mr Chelios.'

'His spirits were *up*,' the lawyer repeated. 'In fact, on the day he called me about the divorce, he asked me to establish contact with the oncology departments at both the Sloan-Kettering Hospital and John Hopkins Hospital.'

'What for?'

'To determine whether there were any experimental treatments for liver cancer. This man wanted to *live*,' Chelios added.

'Move to strike,' said Mullaney. 'It's narrative —'

'This is opinion testimony,' Kuzak put in.

John Gates cut them both off. He sounded angry now, 'Both of you – don't let me have to warn you again.' He sat back. 'The testimony is allowed.'

Newell Cook concealed a little smirk, as he faced the witness again. 'So you don't believe the defendant's opinion that Mr Davis took his own life.'

'The defendant is lying,' Chelios said; then glanced down into the Court and nodded unctuously. 'I'm sorry, Rikki – but you're lying.'

'Objection!' yelled Mullaney.

'Move to strike!' cried Kuzak, like a double-act.

'Sustained,' Judge Gates said, as though reluctantly. 'The last remark is stricken.'

'I have nothing further,' said Newell Cook.

As Mullaney got slowly to his feet, an excited buzz spread across the Courtroom. His voice was a measured drawl, 'Do you have any psychiatric training, Mr Chelios?'

'No, I do not.'

'Have you got any clinical or educational training that would allow you to determine whether or not a person is suicidal?'

'I knew Mr Davis. And —'

'Answer my question, sir,' Mullaney cut in.

Chelios sucked in his breath. 'I have no formal training,' he said at last.

'And when people take their own lives,' Mullaney went on, 'it's often a shock to everyone round them, isn't it?'

Newell Cook jumped up, 'Objection!'

'Sustained,' said Gates.

Mullaney leaned down and whispered urgently to Kuzak; then turned and said, 'We have nothing further, Your Honour.'

Judge Gates nodded and looked at Prosecution, 'Mr Cook?'

'People call as its last witness – Mr David Shaeffer.'

As Newell Cook spoke the name, the buzz across the Court became a low roar. Mullaney was half out of his chair, his face taut with anxiety. 'Objection!' he began; but Kuzak got in before him:

'Move for a continuance – this is a complete surprise, Your Honour.' Kuzak sounded thoroughly alarmed.

'He's on our witness list,' said Cook.

'They put a hundred people on their witness list,' Kuzak

snapped back. 'The chance of this man being called was never a reality – he's up on the same charges.'

'Mr Kuzak,' Judge Gates growled, 'he *is* on their list.' He nodded at Newell Cook. 'You can call the witness. I'll give you all an hour's recess.'

Kuzak and Mullaney looked at each other; then Kuzak leaned over to Rikki Davis and said, 'We gotta talk to you. Outside – in the witness-room.'

*

'What's going on?' Rikki said.

Kuzak was pacing the floor. 'Son of a bitch,' he muttered, without looking at her.

'Your friend, Shaeffer, had to cut a deal,' Mullaney said to her. 'If he's testifying, he *had* to cut *something*.'

Kuzak turned and faced the girl, his voice hard and worried, 'Rikki, if you've been keeping *anything* from us, you gotta come clean now. What could Shaeffer say?'

'Nothing.' Her voice was ice-cold. 'He's innocent. We're both innocent.'

'What about when you broke up?' Mullaney said. 'This Shaeffer guy got an axe to grind?'

Rikki Davis hesitated. 'He was hurt – yes. But so what. He can't testify to anything – except to the fact that I was an unfaithful wife.'

Kuzak took a step towards her. 'Rikki, if we're not prepped for him, this could kill us. So think hard.' He leaned down, so close to her that he could smell the clean dusky scent of her hair. 'Does he have any information of use to them?'

Rikki Davis sat back and tossed her head; her voice was

193

sharp with frustration. 'There isn't any information for him to have, Michael.'

Kuzak straightened up and looked wearily at his colleague. Tommy just shrugged.

*

The man lived up to all that had been promised in Mullaney's slide-show, which Abby and C.J. Lamb had so scoffingly admired. Tall, broad-shouldered, blond and beautiful: a true 'hunk' of bronzed beefcake, the perfect specimen of Californian family-wrecking beachboy, and about as original as a stick of candyfloss at a fairground.

'Could you state your full name for the record, please,' Newell Cook asked him.

'David Allen Shaeffer.'

'And, Mr Shaeffer, could you state your relationship with the defendant, Ms Rikki Davis?'

'Between the period of February 1990 and October 1990, we were lovers.' If the hunk was nervous, he wasn't showing it.

'You knew, during this period of time,' Cook went on, that she was married to Mr Harold Davis?'

'Yes, I did. In fact, it was Mr Davis who introduced us. I worked for the architect who designed their Malibu beach house.'

'During your relationship with the defendant, did she ever discuss leaving her husband?'

'She refused to even consider that,' Shaeffer said; adding, as though to cover his wounded vanity. 'I think it was because of the pre-nup.'

'Objection,' Kuzak and Mullaney said in chorus.

194

'Sustained,' Judge Gates turned to the witness. 'Never mind what you *think*, Mr Shaeffer. Just tell us what you know.'

Newell Cook said to Shaeffer, 'Sir, I call your attention to the day of August 19th 1990. Were you with the defendant on that date?'

'Yes I was. We had gone to brunch at the Mirabelle Restaurant on Sunset. After that, we went back to the house in Beverly Hills. That's when we discovered the body.'

'Mr Davis' body?' said Cook.

'Yes, sir. He was hanging from the ceiling in his bedroom.'

'What'd you do?'

'We tried briefly to get him down but . . . well, he was clearly dead. So we called the police. They came and . . . three days later they arrested Rikki and me and charged us with the crime.'

'Did you have anything to do with this man's death, Mr Shaeffer?'

'No, I did not.'

'To your knowledge,' said Newell Cook, 'did Rikki Davis have anything to do with his death?'

The man hesitated for a second. 'I certainly didn't believe so at first' – he shifted uncomfortably, his brown beach-boy's eyes straying uneasily downwards – 'But, now . . . well, I think she did.'

A great roar, like surf breaking, rolled across the Courtroom. Rikki Davis sat bolt upright, her mouth suddenly opening in blank amazement. Beside her, Kuzak and Mullaney looked almost too stunned to react.

Newell Cook went smoothly on, 'I want you to tell us why, Mr Shaeffer.'

'Objection,' Kuzak said, collecting himself. 'This man's opinion—'

'Overruled,' Gates growled; he turned and repeated to the witness, 'Tell us *why*, Mr Shaeffer.'

The man's voice was firm and confident, 'First off – Rikki had been acting strange all week. She claimed it was because her husband was upset over the cancer. But she seemed unusually jumpy.'

'What else?' said Cook.

'The second thing is . . . well, she'd never bring me back to the house in Beverly Hills. Never. But this day . . . it was very important that I go with her. I think it was to establish an alibi.'

'*Objection!*' Kuzak and Mullaney yelled together.

Judge Gates ignored them. He looked again at the witness and said, 'Again, Sir, just tell us what you *know*. Keep your thoughts to yourself.'

Newell Cook said, 'Anything else, Mr Shaeffer.'

'Yes. About a week before that day, I was riding with her in the car. She stopped by one of the ready tellers to get some cash. And I noticed a book in the backseat – with a bookmark in it.'

'Did you open this book?' Cook asked.

'I did. It was a book about knots.'

'Excuse me?'

'All kinds of rope knots. And the page that was marked – it was a chapter on bunt-line knots.'

'Bunt-line knots?' Cook enquired.

Shaeffer shrugged. 'Yeah, it meant nothing to me at the time. But three weeks ago, my lawyer asked me to go through all the police reports on my arrest. And that's when

I saw that the knot on the cord – the one used to hang Mr Davis – was identified as a bunt-line knot.'

There was another stirring, rumbling sound across the Court; and Rikki Davis leaned over and whispered something urgently to Kuzak, who nodded, frowning.

'Mr Shaeffer,' Cook went on. 'You're giving testimony in exchange for charges against you being dropped. Isn't that right?'

Shaeffer lowered his head a fraction. 'Yes,' he said softly.

'So it could be argued that you're highly motivated to help the Prosecution here – yes?'

Shaeffer wrinkled his smooth, tanned brow. 'But I'm telling the truth. I didn't want to believe it —' He raised his head suddenly, his big eyes opening wide with a kind of childish emotion, 'Hey, I *loved* this woman! But I can't ignore the facts,' he added guilelessly.

Newell Cook nodded. 'Thank you, Mr Shaeffer. That's all.'

A tense silence followed him back to his seat. After a pause, Mullaney hauled himself to his feet. His voice was steady, easy-going, deceptive:

'Now let's see, Mr Shaeffer – according to your testimony here, you had all the pieces to this puzzle three weeks ago. Why didn't you speak up then?'

'I *did*!' Shaeffer cried. 'The District Attorney didn't want to make a deal until yesterday!'

Mullaney pulled a long, sour face, 'Because it finally dawned on him how much his case stinks.'

'Mr Mullaney,' Gates said reprovingly. 'You're really pushing me!'

This time Mullaney ignored the Judge. 'Let's cut to the bone, Mr Shaeffer,' he went on. 'Yesterday, you were up on murder charges. Today, you're a free man in exchange for this ridiculous story.'

'I'm telling the truth.' Shaeffer said stiffly.

'Sure you are,' Mullaney drawled, 'Why would you lie? Just to avoid ending up in the gas-chamber? *Naaah!* – he gave a savage, dismissive gesture, as Newell Cook cut in:

'Move to strike that . . .!'

'Withdrawn,' Mullaney said wearily. 'No further use for this witness.' He began to sit down, as Kuzak sprung to his feet:

'Just a minute, Your Honour – *I* have a couple more questions for this witness. Mr Sheaffer, was this Rikki Davis' car you were talking about? Or a *family* car?'

Shaeffer shrugged. 'It was the one she drove most of the time.'

'To your knowledge – did Mr Davis ever drive it?'

'Yes.'

Kuzak nodded. 'And, Mr Shaeffer, did you ever have occasion to go sailing with Harold Davis?'

'Yes.'

'In fact, he was an avid sailor – was he not?'

'He seemed to be,' Shaeffer said, shrugging again.

'The book you found in the back seat,' Kuzak said. 'The title was *Nautical Knots* – isn't that right?'

'I don't know.'

'It was,' Kuzak said.

'Objection,' said Cook.

'Sustained,' said Judge Gates. 'Mr Kuzak's remark is stricken – he can't offer evidence.'

Kuzak continued, 'It's possible that the book belonged to *Mister* Davis – isn't it, Mr Shaeffer?'

'*She* was the one who drove that car, mostly. So —'

'It's possible that the book was his – isn't it?' Kuzak persisted.

'Yeah – I guess it's possible.'

'Thank you,' Kuzak said; and returned, grim-faced, to his seat beside Mullaney and Rikki Davis.

Chapter Twenty One

Kuzak's office was dark. The floor and most of the furniture were stacked and strewn with files, papers, documents, law books, and old cups of coffee and piled ashtrays. The place smelled like a dead poker game.

Mullaney was sprawled out in exhausted sleep on the sofa, his shoes off, one hand hanging limply to the floor; while Mike Kuzak dozed, his head on the desk, a thermos flask and empty cup at his elbow.

Suddenly the door crashed open and C.J. Lamb strode in – wide-awake, cool and sharp, in her beautifully fitting suit – holding up a sheaf of big glossy photographs in her hand.

'Your early call, gentlemen!' she cried, dumping the photographs on the desk in front of Kuzak. 'Your lovely attorney, Chelios, has been dating the victim's daughter – Marion Davis.'

Kuzak stared blearily at her. 'What —?'

'The one who was cut out of the will,' C.J. said briskly; she spread the photos across the desk and pointed to several. 'These are from two nights ago,' she added. 'And this is last night – it's definitely her.'

Behind them, Mullaney had come lurching across the

room. 'What the hell could this mean?' he said, rubbing his sore eyes and examining the photos over C.J.'s shoulder.

'Maybe nothing,' she said. 'But if not, it sure makes for one hell of a coincidence.'

'Tommy,' Kuzak said, 'call Stuart and get him in here right away!'

'It's nearly midnight,' Tommy protested wearily.

'Wake him up,' Kuzak turned to C.J., speaking rapidly now. 'Mark Chelios' office building keeps video tape records of everyone who goes in and out' – he glanced across at Mullaney – 'Isn't that right, Tommy?'

'Paltech Security,' Mullaney yawned. 'I got a buddy who works there. He told me.'

'They're supposed to keep the tapes for thirty days before they erase,' said Kuzak. 'I want somebody to get those tapes, then everyone in the office – the whole damn firm, if necessary – is going to go right through them. Tommy – call your friend at Paltech and get him to fix it. We put Mr Chelios back on the stand,' he added triumphantly.

Mullaney stood rubbing his midnight-shadow. 'Lemme take him, Michael. I'll pop the puss right out of him!'

'No, Tommy. This one's mine. *I'm* going to get him.'

*

Mark Chelios, attorney to the rich and famous, was on the stand, spruce and sleek in a lemon-coloured sports jacket, knife-edged khaki trousers and white loafers, his black hair shining like laquer in the reflected glare of the TV lights.

'Mr Chelios' – Mike Kuzak's voice was flat, without menace – 'you previously stated that you drafted Mr Davis's most recent will.'

201

'That is correct.'

Kuzak held up a stiff document. 'I'll show you this and ask if you recognise it?' A Court official took the paper and handed it up to the witness.

Chelios examined it quickly and said, 'It's a memo dictated by me after we executed the will.'

'Could you please read Paragraph Three, for the record?' Kuzak asked him.

Chelios unfolded the document and began to read, clearly, fluently, as though he knew it by heart:

"Mr Davis, indicating his accord with the provisions contained therein, executed his signature as testator. I then affixed my signature as witness to the foregoing. Mr Davis then confirmed to Julia Delaney that the testator's signature was in fact his and Ms Delaney then affixed her signature as the second witness.'

'You say that Mr Davis confirmed to Julia Delaney that the signature was in fact *his*. Didn't she *see* him sign the will?'

'What? Well' – Chelios hesitated – 'I'm sure she did.'

'Then, why would he have to tell her what she saw?' Kuzak pressed him.

'I'm not really sure. This was many months ago.'

Kuzak now held up a single sheet of paper. 'I have here a signed declaration of Ms Delaney' – he passed the document to a Court official – 'It was obtained from her this morning and I offer it to the Court. She states that she was not in the room when Mr Davis signed. That's why he had to *tell* her it was his signature.'

'Well, so what?' Chelios frowned. 'There's no question he signed it or —'

'The actual signing of this will,' Kuzak broke in, 'was *not* witnessed by two people – was it, Mr Chelios?'

'I'm not positive,' Chelios paused. His face was glossy with sweat. 'I guess maybe it wasn't,' he added, glancing nervously around him.

'And what does that fact do to the validity of the will, Mr Chelios?'

'Technically' – the attorney hesitated again, cleared his throat – 'technically, it makes it invalid.'

'Yes. Then how would the estate be probated?'

'Mr Davis would be deemed to have died intestate.'

'Meaning that he died leaving no will?'

'But it doesn't matter,' Chelios said quickly. 'If a spouse dies intestate, California Law says the bulk of the estate goes to the surviving spouse. So Rikki Davis would still be the main beneficiary.'

'Very true,' Kuzak said, nodding. 'But if Rikki Davis is convicted of murder, she would be disqualified. And without a valid will, the Cancer Society is out. Who would the money go to under California Law, Mr Chelios?'

'Surviving children.'

'Which would be who in this case?'

'His only child is the daughter, Marion Davis.'

'So Marion Davis – that woman right *there* –' Kuzak had turned, indicating the blonde woman sitting very erect and pale in the well of the Court – 'she stands to inherit everything if my client is convicted. Isn't that right, Mr Chelios?'

'Yes.'

'So *she* would have a motive to kill Mr Davis and frame Rikki, wouldn't she?'

203

'I doubt very much that she would be well versed in the validity of wills,' Chelios said evasively.

'She would,' said Kuzak, 'if a very clever lawyer, with inside information, were advising her.' The lawyer on the stand didn't move a muscle, didn't even blink. 'Mr Chelios,' Kuzak went on, 'do you have a social relationship with Marion Davis?'

'Objection!' Newell Cook cried.

'Overruled,' said Judge Gates.

Kuzak repeated the question, 'Do you have a social relationship with Marion Davis?'

Chelios hesitated, his voice missing a beat. '. . . We've had dinner together,' he said at last; his tone was almost indifferent.

Mullaney stood up and casually passed one of the photographs on the Defence table to Newell Cook. At the same time, Kuzak handed a copy up to Chelios.

'Mr Chelios,' Kuzak said, 'I show you a picture taken two nights ago. Would that be you and Marion together?'

The photograph in Chelios' hand was completely steady. 'Yes,' he replied.

'Would you describe for the Court what the two of you are doing in that photograph,' Kuzak said.

'We're kissing.'

The stir across the Court rose to a crescendo, and this time the excitement spread as far as Judge Gates, who bent down and made a display of fingering the documents on his desk, to conceal his expression of delight.

Kuzak allowed a long pause to let the information have its full impact on the Jury, before he went on, 'How long have you been seeing Marion?'

Newell Cook was on his feet again, addressing the Judge, 'Your Honour. Short recess, please.'

'Siddown,' Gates growled; he turned to the witness, repeating Kuzak's question: 'How long?'

'About eight months,' Chelios said, head bowed.

Kuzak acknowledged the Judge's welcome interjection; then, retrieving control of the questioning, said, 'And, Mr Chelios, Miss Davis knew the will would be declared invalid, didn't she? All she had to do was to challenge it.'

'Marion could never have killed her father,' Chelios said, with a flush of defiance.

Kuzak pressed relentlessly on. 'You purposely saw to it that it was invalid so that Harold Davis would die intestate – didn't you, Mr Chelios? *Because you loved Marion Davis.* Isn't that right, sir?'

The witness looked boldly at Newell Cook. 'I'm asserting my Fifth Amendment rights. I refuse to answer any more questions.'

'That's okay,' Kuzak said. 'I haven't *got* any more questions.'

There was a low rumble of approval across the Court, as Kuzak returned to his seat.

Judge Gates looked down happily at Newell Cook; he was beginning to enjoy himself hugely. 'Mr Cook?'

'Nothing, Your Honour.'

'You may step down, sir,' Judge Gates told Chelios. 'Defence will call its next witness.'

As Chelios returned to his place, Mullaney leaned over and muttered in Kuzak's ear, 'Let's stop right here, Mike!'

'What?' Kuzak stared at him. Mullaney continued, in a low excited whisper:

'I don't care who we put up there, Michael. Forensics –

the shrink – even Rikki. We will *never* have more momentum than we got right now.'

'Mr Kuzak!' Judge Gates called impatiently, interrupting them both.

'One second, Your Honour' – Kuzak turned back to Mullaney. '*You serious?*'

'Michael, you just dropped a bomb,' Tommy said; he was still whispering, louder, more insistently now. '*Let's get the Jury back in there deliberating while the room's still shakin'!*'

Kuzak shrugged, reluctantly. 'Your ready to close, Tommy?' he said, out loud.

'Yes.'

Kuzak glanced once at his partner, before standing up and addressing the Bench. 'Your Honour. The Defence rests.'

The noise in the Court was now one of noisy confusion. Judge Gates had to bang twice for order, before nodding to Kuzak. 'Closing arguments – two o'clock. We're adjourned.'

*

'So we're not going out to lunch, Leland?' Rosalind Shays stood in the middle of McKenzie's office, clasping her big handbag to her hips, looking at him with her immaculately plucked eyebrows slightly raised.

He looked back at her, solemnly, through his bifocals. 'Well – I thought we'd talk here, first.'

Rosalind's eyebrows went up another fraction, as she waited. Leland cleared his throat a couple of times, paused, smiled at her and began, 'Rosalind. I've been very happy with you. You —'

'You don't have to preface anything, Leland. Your answer is "no".'

'I don't love you,' McKenzie said quietly.

Rosalind stared blankly at him. After a pause, he continued, 'I realize I may never meet *anybody* again who I'll come to love. But it would be wrong to marry you out of default.'

'Do you think – in time – you might love me?'

'No.'

'Did you ever think I could be so ridiculous?'

'You're not ridiculous,' he smiled miserably.

'You have no idea how scared I was that night in the restaurant. Before I asked you. I even practised it.'

'You don't know how close I was to saying "Yes".'

'So.' She paused. 'What do we do now?'

'I don't want to stop seeing you,' he said, struggling to sound calm and compassionate at the same time.

'I guess it would be stupid for us *not* to. I mean, at our age . . .' she smiled, almost shyly. 'We enjoy each other's company and, well, love is for the young, right?' Rosalind paused, waiting for McKenzie's reaction; but McKenzie said nothing.

'Okay,' she said, defeated. She glanced hurriedly at her watch. 'Listen. Let's skip lunch. I've got some errands and' – she paused again – 'we're still on for dinner, right?'

'Sure.'

'Maybe Italian tonight. I feel like pasta.' She gave him a bright false smile.

He nodded. 'Okay.'

She smiled again, almost concealing her misery. 'You're right, Leland. This is the right thing. See you later on.'

Leland McKenzie watched her leave, less able to mask his

own pain. But his expression was resolute, his mind made up. He was not the Senior Partner of Mackenzie Brackman for nothing.

Chapter Twenty Two

The atmosphere in the Criminal Court was as charged as if shot through with high-voltage static electricity. Even the voices of Counsel seemed to crackle with suppressed emotion.

Tommy Mullaney was on his feet, for his closing argument. He had his own emotions under tight wraps, his voice friendly, easy-going – giving no hint that each of his words held the beautiful Rikki Davis' life in the balance.

'I don't know about you, folks, but I'm more confused than when we first started. Let's just start with what we *do* know for sure. First – all the physical evidence, *all* of it, could be consistent with suicide. Their star Homicide Detective told you under oath.' From the corner of his eye, Mullaney noticed Jonathan Rollins slip into the Courtroom and take his place just behind him at the defendant's table.

Mullaney paused. Rollins began to whisper to him; then handed him some photographs and a print-out from Chelios' office security.

'Just a moment, Your Honour.' Mullaney and Rollins began whispering excitedly. Tommy nodded finally and faced the Court again.

'The main thing against Rikki Davis,' he went on, keeping his excitement well under control, 'was motive. She was supposedly the only one with motive. The witness who was *selling* that – was the attorney, Mark Chelios. Then, suddenly, it turns out that's all wrong. The will was invalid, the *daughter* stands to get everything if – *if* she can get Rikki disqualified with a murder conviction. And she knew this. She knew 'cause she was sleeping with guess who? Mr Chelios, the lawyer who carefully arranged for the will to *be* invalid. What a scheme. Wow!' Mullaney paused for his words to have their full effect.

'Well, people,' he went on, 'right now I don't know – maybe Marion Davis killed her father for the money, maybe the guy really *did* commit suicide. I can't know. The Prosecution? They *definitely* don't know. They're over there suddenly dropping charges against the boyfriend, David Shaeffer. One day he's up on a First Degree, next day he's not. They don't have a clue what's going on. What a mess. Reasonable doubt all over. What a terrible mess.' He turned, with a wide empty gesture of contempt, towards Newell Cook. 'You better clear things up,' he added.

*

Newell Cook now rose, his face slightly pale under his tan. He looked at Judge Gates, then at the Jury, and began:

'The defendant's a wealthy woman who hired the best lawyers money could buy and they've done everything possible to confuse you. And they're good. These lawyers are *very* good,' he nodded with self-deprecating irony.

'But let's reduce this thing to the basic facts. Rikki Davis had a twenty-six million dollar motive. Rikki Davis'

210

fingerprints were found on the cord that was used to hang the victim. She has no alibi. Her own lover concluded she had to have done it. There was a book describing how to make the knot that was tied around the victim's head. That book was seen in her car. Common sense, ladies and gentlemen. Rikki Davis killed her husband. Mr Mullaney may be confused. But I'm not. Nor should you be.'

Newell Cook nodded to the Judge and returned quietly to his seat.

*

There was standing room only in the Court. Most of the spectators, attorneys, reporters and TV crews had been waiting for less than an hour, when the word went breathlessly round the packed benches that the Jury were coming back.

There was a deathly hush, as though several hundred pairs of lungs were cramped, hardly daring to breathe out. Judge Gates showed no emotion, as he watched the twelve citizens file into the box; then said:

'Mr Foreman – the Jury has reached a verdict?'

'Yes, Your Honour.'

'How do you find?'

'We, the Jury, in the matter of the People versus Rikki Davis, on the charge of First Degree Murder – find the defendant . . . not guilty.'

The whole Court exploded with a deafening roar – a combined cacophony of yelling, cheering, shrieking, boo-ing and clapping, while flash-guns flared like lightning, and there was a small stampede of reporters heading for the doors.

211

Judge Gates was hammering furiously for silence, while Rikki Davis stood chastely hugging Tommy Mullaney, then – perhaps less chastely – Kuzak, who broke away, to shake hands with her, then with Mullaney, who was grey and burnt-out with exhaustion.

Judge Gates was just managing to make himself heard. 'Members of the Jury, we're done. Thank you for your service. I hope you enjoyed it.' He gave an impish grin, as he stood up. 'I know I did!'

*

Kuzak closed the door against the continuing pandamonium of the Courtroom, shutting out a barrage of reporters and TV cameramen. He nodded at Mullaney, 'They got a Press Room set up – you start with 'em, Tommy. We'll be in in a minute.'

Rikki Davis had dropped into a chair; she'd removed her dark glasses and now sat smiling round her. Her eyes glowed. 'I'm absolutely numb,' she gasped.

'You should be,' said Kuzak. 'You pulled it off.'

Her smile faded into a frown. 'What do you mean – *I pulled it off?*'

Mullaney had slipped back out to talk to the Press, and she was left alone now with Kuzak. He stood and nodded grimly down at her. 'Too easy, Rikki.' His eyes locked on to hers: but there was no triumph, not even relief in his expression. He said slowly, 'It just fell together a little too neatly.'

Her lips parted. She gaped at him. 'What are you talking about?' she said at last.

'I'm talking about you and Mark Chelios.' Kuzak was

still holding the photos and print-out that Rollins had just handed Mullaney in Court. 'We got hold of these,' he went on. 'The videotaped security recordings of his office building. You've been in there twice during the last month. We've also been running your message units. You've called him three times during the trial.'

Her lovely mouth sagged open like a torn pocket. 'So?' she murmured.

'*You two* killed your husband. Not you and David Shaeffer. You and Mark Chelios. You either did it yourselves, or you had it done.'

'That's absurd,' she said automatically.

'I don't think so,' Kuzak said. 'Mark Chelios is a brilliant lawyer. The screw-up on the will was a mistake even a rookie attorney wouldn't make. He did that to give the daughter a motive. He *romanced* Marion Davis to set her up and to set *himself* up to be impeached on the witness stand.'

The din from the Courtroom outside seemed to have suddenly subsided. It was very quiet in the Witness Room. 'I've completely lost you now,' Rikki said, with a forced smile.

Kuzak shook his head. 'Oh, you follow me all right – you follow me *exactly*. You both knew there was no way Harold Davis could *possibly* be murdered without suspicion falling directly on you. You could *try* to stage the suicide – sure – but that would be fifty-fifty at best. The only way to guarantee your getting away with it – was double jeopardy. To be tried and acquitted.'

She sat listening to him with a cold, insolent expression, but said nothing. Kuzak went on:

'So Mark Chelios set himself up as the big witness against you, the guy who could prove motive. Then he put the memo in the files and gave the files to us. He kissed Marion Davis when he *had* to know we were following her. He knew we'd blow him up on the stand – and thereby blow up the Prosecution's case. You insisted that we tail the daughter, you insisted that we tail Chelios. Perfect.'

She blinked at him. Then said, almost indifferently, 'Why would he take the stand and make himself a suspect?'

Kuzak shrugged. 'Probably because he has an air-tight alibi. Maybe because he knew *you* made all the arrangements and nothing could be traced to him if he were actually investigated.

She looked at him for a moment, then suddenly smiled. 'It's a nice story, Counsellor. Too bad you can't repeat it.'

'Sometimes I forget my ethical obligations,' he replied, with genuine menace.

She stared up at him, the colour beginning to seep back into her cheeks. 'You got two choices here,' she told him at last. 'There's a big Press conference going on outside. You can walk in there, with a long face, and say you were completely duped by your client.' She stood up. 'Or you can say nothing. Just be the brilliant star Defence Attorney that the whole country now knows you to be. A winner or a loser – it's up to you, Michael.' She smiled brilliantly at him and turned. 'I believe I'm free to go now.'

He said nothing, as she walked nonchalantly out of the room. He felt he needed a drink.

*

It was another day, another Morning Conference, in the offices of McKenzie Brackman and Partners. Douglas

214

Brackman glowered down the table, noting at once that C.J. Lamb was absent.

'All right. First up – I note that C.J., who is late *again* – has brought up another significant client, *again*. German Motor Works is opening up an American Division and she has evidently snagged them.'

Arnie Becker suppressed a yawn. 'Good old C.J.,' he drawled, mimicking her English accent.

Brackman ignored him. 'Next up – Recklaw versus Sinai Hospital . . . Victor?'

Sifuentes nodded: 'We represent Kate Recklaw – suing for damages caused by an unnecessary hysterectomy —'

They all looked up, as C.J. came breathlessly in, clutching her files and looking unusually ruffled, even distressed.

'It's all right, guys! – *this* time I really do have an excuse!' She smiled round her and dropped limply into her chair. 'I've been stuck in the bloody lift for thirty minutes,' she added, and paused, breathing heavily. Then she gave Brackman a brave smile; 'You better get it looked at, Douglas – or you'll have a nasty lawsuit on your hands.'

Brackman cleared his throat and said pompously, 'Which brings us to an administrative item. Besides elevator mishaps, the electrical difficulties in the building have caused some power surges which have shot down many of our word-processing facilities . . .'

A dull groan went up round the table. All the drama and glamour of a great law firm in action, still basking in the after-glory of the Rikki Davis trial, was reduced, by the ineffable Brackman, to trivial details about electrical power surges and shut-down computers.

Not a word of sympathy for C.J., whom he now began

addressing, 'C.J. – you've got the German company? This is a fact?'

'I'm meeting with the C.E.O.,' she said, nodding, 'and four vice-presidents, on Friday. Looks like a go.'

'Fantastic' – Brackman turned briskly to McKenzie, at his side. 'And Leland, you're meeting with Rosalind Shays over Velnick's lease with Tammon. Yes?'

'Tonight,' McKenzie said.

Brackman nodded. 'Adjourned,' he said, and stood up. Still not a word of sympathy for C.J. – let alone an apology, for her being trapped in a black steel cell for half an hour . . . *Just as well*, she thought grimly, *I'm a forgiving girl who doesn't suffer from claustrophobia.*

*

Leland McKenzie and Rosalind Shays were mature, experienced human beings who knew how to control their emotions, and not to allow such complications to damage their professional relationship.

That night, anybody seeing them coming out of McKenzie's office, on their way to the lifts, would have taken them both for two detached, highly-motivated legal executives, insulated from each other by the exacting pressures of their respective careers.

The appearance was utterly false. They were both distressed, even miserable, although each was trying valiantly to conceal the fact. McKenzie was holding the door open for her, as she stepped out of the office complex, apparently preoccupied with legal niceties, saying, 'I think it's a mistake just to capitulate on the tax abatements.'

'There's no point,' McKenzie replied briskly, 'wasting the time of six attorneys, fighting over a moot point.'

'It's *not* a moot point, Leland,' she snapped, as she let the glass doors swing shut behind them. 'It's a contingency,' she added irritably. 'It's what any good lawyer plans for.'

She began to stride across the reception area towards the lifts, with McKenzie padding behind her. Suddenly he stopped. 'Rosalind . . .'

She had reached the lifts, when he added, 'Rosalind – I'm sorry I can't marry you.'

She paused for a moment, punching the call button of the lift. 'This isn't about that, Leland – I'm making a legal point.'

'It *is* about that, Rosalind. For the last week, I've been getting nothing from you but resentment and argument. You know that's true,' he added, speaking to her turned back, as she stood resolutely waiting for the lift.

Rosalind Shays sighed, without turning. 'I don't resent you, Leland,' she said quietly, speaking to the lift door. 'If anything, I resent *myself*.'

'For staying with a man who doesn't love you?' McKenzie asked wretchedly, as the lift arrived.

This time she did turn, as the lift door slid open behind her. 'I really don't want to talk about it,' she said; and before he could speak, she'd turned again and walked through the open lift door. Only the lift itself wasn't there. Instead, just a black steel wall leading down into a cold black shaft.

McKenzie was aware of a short, horrible, echoing scream, then silence. He reacted automatically. He shouted, twice, 'Rosalind, Rosalind!' But although his vocal chords still operated, the rest of his body was paralysed.

217

'Oh my God!' he cried, '*Oh my God!*'
There was no sound from the empty shaft.

OTHER LA LAW NOVELS PUBLISHED BY BOXTREE

A FAIR TRIAL
Charles Butler

A young and successful advertising executive has a head-on collision with another car, killing a mother and her son. When a journalist finds out that Carlton had committed a drink-driving offence only recently, the media close in for the kill.

ISBN: 1-85283-606-7

THE PARTNERSHIP
Charles Butler

The same night that Arnie Becker is confined to a police cell after a drug bust at a yuppie beach party, Leland McKenzie collapses and is rushed to hospital. Things couldn't get much worse for the thriving L.A. Law firm.

ISBN: 1-85283-606-6

INTO THE DARK
Charles Butler

Grace Van Owen is taken on to fight a large chemical firm and win compensation for a little girl who was blinded when she crashed her bike on wasteland – one of the corporation's dumpsites.

ISBN: 1-85283-607-5

A WOMAN SCORNED
Julie Robitaille

Rosalind Shays, former senior partner at MBCK, decides to sue the L.A. law firm over her unfair dismissal. Every move in this battle of wits is vital . . . the future of the partnership is at stake.

ISBN: 1-85283-602-4

COLD BLOOD
Charles Butler

Elsa Chandler admits to shooting her husband. Grace Van Owen is determined to prove that, although the physical evidence points to a case of premeditated murder, all is not what it seems.

ISBN: 1-85283-699-7